MURDER AS SWEET AS HONEY

DIANA ORGAIN

Lemonade
Press

OTHER TITLES BY DIANA ORGAIN

MATERNAL INSTINCTS MYSTERY SERIES

Bundle of Trouble - FREE The only thing tougher than solving a murder... giving birth!

Motherhood is Murder Kate joins a new mom group where mischief and murder run rampant.

Formula for Murder A hit and run crash catapults Kate into a mystery at the French Consulate.

Nursing a Grudge Kate's budding PI business is threatened when a new PI poaches her client.

Pampered to Death Spa day has never been so deadly!

Killer Cravings Can Kate juggle being a PI, pregnant and those cravings all at the same time?

A Deathly Rattle Who shot rival PI, Vicente Domingo?

Rockabye Murder Dancing can be murder—literally.

Prams & Poison Are there too many skeletons in the Victorian closet Paula's is renovating?

LOVE OR MONEY MYSTERY SERIES

A First Date with Death Reality TV meets murder!

A Second Chance at Murder Georgia's new boyfriend disappears in the Pyrenees Mountains.

Third Time's a Crime If only love were as simple as murder…

CHAPTER 1

*V*icki Lawson pulled into the parking lot three minutes late. That was fashionably late, right? She took a breath as she grabbed her wicker basket of samples.

"Breathe," she whispered. "This will go great."

She'd known it was a long shot when she dialed the phone number on the flyer. After last year's debacle, she hadn't expected to get a booth at the Fall Festival—Julia, the festival chair, had absolutely hated Mona's jam and Vicki's honey and had sent them packing. Her exact words had been something like, "You'll get a booth here over my dead body."

But Vicki had decided to try again this year—she and her best friend, Mona, *needed* a venue to sell their products while Jammin' Honey was being rebuilt. If Vicki could move some of her products at the Fall Festival, she'd buy herself—and her dwindling savings account—a little more time.

And the long shot might be about to pay off. When Vicki had called, she'd found out that Julia wasn't the festival chair this year, and that the new chair would be delighted to take a look at Vicki's samples.

Vicki opened the car door and headed toward the warehouse.

The exterior of the warehouse looked festival ready. Straw bales and pumpkins lined the outside, alongside a few scarecrows. Some leaves were scattered by the entrance, and a large sign on the roof announced the dates of the festival.

Pretty good advertising, Vicki thought. *I feel festive already!*

Then Vicki caught sight of Julia near the corner of the building.

Less festive, now. What's she doing here?

Julia was tall, with chestnut hair and an impeccable sense of fashion. Today, her hair was pulled back into a ponytail, and her belted coat and skinny jeans looked effortlessly put together. But Vicki only had time to feel a flash of envy at Julia's sartorial sensibilities.

Something wasn't right.

Julia was gesticulating wildly, arguing with an older man. By the time Vicki drew near the door, the man had stormed off. Julia whirled around and caught sight of Vicki, and her face reddened.

"Hey, Vicki," Julia called, striding toward her.

Vicki paused, unsure what to do. Why was Julia even here if she wasn't the festival chair?

"Um . . ." Julia reached her. "That was my stepdad. He wants to sell his paintings at the festival."

"Oh." Vicki opened the door halfway. "I thought Kristen was coordinating it this year."

Julia glowered. "She is, but I'm the deputy chair. And I won't have his paintings here. They're not very good, and he prices them way too high."

Vicki stayed where she was and let the door swing closed. *Julia seems . . . really upset.* Despite her profound dislike for the woman, a kernel of sympathy bloomed in her chest.

"He kept saying these paintings were different, that he'd price them reasonably and that he wasn't as protective of them, but I know how he is about his stupid art. I can't have him in the festival," Julia said. "We can't be responsible for them. If one of his paintings got damaged or stolen . . . well, he'd have a fit."

"That looked like more than a painting issue," said Vicki slowly. "Is everything okay? It seemed pretty heated."

Julia scoffed, but her chin trembled. "Family. You know the drill."

"Family?" Vicki probed.

"My mom's sick." Julia stopped, looking almost surprised that the words had come out of her mouth. "Never mind me and my problems. It's not a big deal. What are you doing here?"

It seemed like a big deal. But Vicki decided to keep that observation to herself. "I'm here to talk to Kristen. She invited me to bring samples over."

Julia looked at the basket, rolled her eyes, and shoved the door open. Vicki followed her inside.

A spacious room opened up before her, the exposed wiring and piping along the ceiling offering a casually trendy ambiance.

Halfway across the space, a flannel-clad woman with braided red hair was laying down some papers, spacing each sheet about ten feet apart. She glanced toward Vicki and Julia and waved.

"Vicki?" she called.

Vicki nodded, then sneezed. The light streaming in from a set of high windows illuminated the floating dust motes.

The woman jogged in her direction and stuck out her hand. "I'm Kristen. Just mapping out vendor stalls. This is our first year in this space, and they let us come in early."

Vicki shook Kristen's hand. "So good to meet you."

Kristen pointed to a nearby table covered in a decade of dust. "Yikes. This place needs a cleaning. But why don't you put your basket there, if you don't mind, and we'll take a look at your samples." Then she glanced quizzically at Julia. "Who was yelling just now?"

"Frank was harassing me again," moaned Julia.

Kristen rested a hand on Julia's upper back, and they stepped away, Kristen's voice becoming soothing.

While they were talking, Vicki placed her baskets on the table and pulled out a handful of sample tins. After a minute, Julia and Kristen returned to the table.

"Here are the samples," Vicki said to Kristen.

Before Kristen could reach them or say anything, Julia snatched a tin of the relaxing body scrub, opened it, and sniffed. She wrinkled her nose and muttered, "I wouldn't put this crap in the festival."

Molten frustration welled up in Vicki's chest. *Well, I wouldn't put your crappy attitude in the festival.*

"Oh!" Kristen's eyes widened, and she snapped her fingers as if she'd forgotten something. "I'm an idiot. Julia, could you run down the street to the bank and get the last five month's transactions for the festival account? I was supposed to print those off this morning. I need to see if a sponsor's check has cleared. They called me up yesterday and asked if I would look into it. It cleared a while ago, but they're old-school, and I want to be able to show them a physical paper trail when they come by this afternoon."

"Fine," huffed Julia. She grabbed her purse and stalked out the door.

As soon as the door closed behind her, Kristen shot Vicki a conspiratorial grin. "That should give us some time."

Vicki smiled back. She liked Kristen's style.

"So, what do we have in the baskets?" asked Kristen. "Well, I assume jam and honey? Julia mentioned something about the honey situation from last year. She . . . can be a bit much, can't she?"

Vicki breathed a sigh of relief and searched for something diplomatic. "I like Julia, but her tastes and mine don't necessarily jive."

Kristen laughed aloud. "My tastes don't jive with Julia's either. I think she just doesn't like jam, to be honest. In the years she ran the festival, she rarely let any vendors sell jam. I, however, enjoy it just fine—and even if I didn't, I'm aware enough to know that someone else might."

Tin by tin, Vicki handed over the samples. She held her breath as Kristen smelled the two body scrubs and tasted Vicki's cinnamon honey and Mona's jam.

"Where do you get your supply of honey?" Kristen asked.

"I have my own beehives," said Vicki, running her thumb along the rim of the wicker basket. Kristen looked impressed, so she added, "I also grow and dry my own herbs."

"This is what I call *good* quality," said Kristen, tucking the last tin back inside the basket. "I would love to have you sell your goods at the Fall Festival."

Yes! Vicki forced herself to maintain a professional grin rather than break out into a disco celebration. "Thank you," she said. "I hope Julia doesn't give you too much grief about that."

Kristen waved a dismissive hand. "Ignore Julia. She's had a tough few years with her family problems. You saw how crazy her stepdad is."

Vicki hesitated. "I don't mean to pry, but . . ."

"But anyone would be curious after the yelling display they put on out there?" Kristen said with a knowing look.

Vicki nodded sheepishly.

"Well"—Kristen glanced back and forth as if to make sure no one was near enough to overhear them, though they were the only two people in the warehouse—"Julia's mom has been very sick for a few years. Julia's stepdad wants her to drop everything and wait on her mother hand and foot. Like, he wants her to stay at home and take care of her mom because it's a *daughter's duty*, or something. Now, Julia isn't an only child. She has a brother who'd be happy to help. But her stepdad insists that it's Julia's job and *only* Julia's job. He's already gone behind Julia's back once and gotten her demoted to second-in-charge of the festival. Even told her afterward that she should have more time to look after her mom now."

"He sounds like a real winner," said Vicki sarcastically. *Might explain why Julia has been so mean. She has her own problems.*

"Julia even offered to pay for a live-in nurse. And it's not like she doesn't see her mom! She's there literally every day—she just doesn't want to spend every single minute there. But the idea that Julia would leave her mom's bedside for even five minutes sends the man into an uproar."

"Wow, you'd think he'd appreciate Julia's offer to pay for a nurse." Vicki picked up the basket.

"You'd think." Kristen tapped her fingers on the table and glared at the door. "But he's crazy. He's so insistent that Julia be at home with her mom that he's threatened to ruin the Fall Festival."

CHAPTER 2

"*M*ona, we're in the festival!" Vicki exclaimed when her best friend answered the phone.

"What? Are you serious?" Mona shrieked.

"Yes, it opens in a couple weeks. I can have a bunch of stuff ready by then. How about you?" Vicki buckled her seat belt and leaned back against the headrest, giddy.

"I should be able to work on some new jams this weekend," said Mona breathlessly. "How about we do a fall theme?"

"You read my mind." Vicki broke out into a dance in her seat. "I already have some cinnamon and pumpkin-spice honey sticks."

"I could make some muscadine jam and apple butter. And some strawberry and blueberry jam to fill out the table."

Vicki's mouth watered. "That sounds delicious! I'll have my body scrubs, some lip balm, and my honey straws. I might take along some honeycomb too. I'll be harvesting tomorrow after Coupon Clippers."

"Mmm, I love your honeycomb. Did you know that beeswax is being sold at some festivals now?"

"Beeswax, huh? Where'd you see that?"

"At the county fair last weekend. The guy selling it had some candles, but also just the plain beeswax. He said people are using it to coat their tools, and cheesemakers use it to cover their cheese."

"Interesting," she said slowly. "Beeswax is the main ingredient in most of my products, but I could bring along a few pieces of plain beeswax too."

"Cool," said Mona. "Oh, could I buy one of your relaxing scrubs? I could sure use all the help I can get to keep my stress levels down. These contractors working on my store are so flaky it might kill me."

"I'll give you a jar," promised Vicki.

"No, that'll cut into your profits."

"It's okay." Vicki grinned, even though Mona couldn't see her. "I'm doing it for a selfish reason."

"Hmm?"

"Because I'd love some of your muscadine jam!"

"Consider it a trade. I'll bring a jar to Coupon Clippers tomorrow!"

They hung up, and Vicki checked an incoming text message. It was from her brother, Leo. *Hey, we still on for dinner?*

Of course, she replied. *See you in a few hours!*

* * *

THE CHILLY AFTERNOON AIR SIGNALED AUTUMN WAS UPON MAGNOLIA Falls. From her barstool perch in her homey kitchen, Vicki squinted down at the glass bowl on the counter. "Let's see . . . just a little more peppermint oil. That should do the trick," she murmured. She unscrewed the bottle of peppermint oil and filled the dropper.

"One, two, three . . ." she whispered, counting each drop.

This was it. She could feel it. Once she put the finishing touches on her line of honey body scrubs, she could really try to make this business work. The Fall Festival would be the first big test.

She glanced out the window, at the beehives on the far side of the yard. Her first venture into the honey business had gone up in flames —literally—when her best friend's store had burned down shortly before the grand opening. Before the fire, Mona had been planning to feature Vicki's products. Now, neither friend had much of a functioning business. Sure, they had online stores, but Vicki's certainly didn't come close to making ends meet.

Her throat tightened at the thought of checking the balance in her savings account.

But these scrubs—and the Fall Festival—were going to be her big break.

I can practically smell the success! Vicki thought.

Or maybe that's just the peppermint.

The peppermint overpowered the kitchen, even masking the spicy smell of the simmering stew on the back burner.

Ventilation!

She opened the window halfway, letting in the crisp, clean air.

From outside came an emphatic *quack*.

Vicki peered down at the grassy lawn. "What's that, Sunny? Is that enough peppermint?"

She picked up the bottle to recap it, but a thin sheen of oil on the glass made it slippery. The tiny jar slipped through her fingers and fell straight into the body scrub mixture. With a little shriek, she snatched it back up and held it up to the light. It didn't look like too much had spilled. But the scrub *definitely* had enough peppermint now.

Sunny, her pet duck, quacked in reply and shook her white tail feathers.

"Good girl!" Vicki closed the bottle securely, then wiped her hands on a navy kitchen towel and reached for the bowl of blueberries she kept close at hand. She tossed a berry out the window, and Sunny swerved to chase it down.

"You're all sunshine, huh?" Vicki had adopted Sunny after her latest romantic interest had ended up in jail for burning down Mona's store and killing someone in the process. Adopting a duck was more of a commitment than any of the standard breakup scripts, like changing her hair or buying pints of Ben & Jerry's by the armful or learning how to swordfight, but Vicki had loved every minute of being a duck mom.

Sunny waddled over to the kitchen window and gazed up hopefully.

Vicki tossed her another blueberry. Then the oven beeped, announcing it was done preheating. She glanced up at the wall clock.

"Your Uncle Leo's going to be here soon!" she said to Sunny. "It's time to put the cornbread in the oven and make the salad."

She opened the preheated oven and set the glass pan of cornbread batter on the rack. Then she grabbed a bagged Caesar salad from the fridge and tossed it.

Turning her attention back to her scrub mixture, she murmured. "Now, where were we?"

She bent over and sniffed the mixture, and the overwhelming scent of peppermint wafted over her. She grabbed a wooden spoon and started stirring. After a couple minutes, she squinted down at the scrub.

"I think that should do it," she said, setting aside the wooden spoon. She glanced out at the yard, but Sunny had wandered back to her makeshift pond in a children's plastic wading pool. With a half sigh, Vicki tapped the edge of the bowl. "Guess I better test this scrub out if I'm going to be giving samples to the coupon queens tomorrow."

She carried the peppermint scrub—she'd call this one her *energizing blend* until she came up with a clever name for it—up the stairs and into the bathroom.

"Self-care, for the win." Vicki set down the bowl and smoothed some of the scrub on her arms. Warmth tingled over her skin.

This feels good.

Her skin got hotter and hotter. Too hot. Vicki let out a yelp and dove for the sink. She turned on the cold water and washed the scrub off her arms.

Still feels a bit tingly. Guess that was too much peppermint oil.

She blew on her arms to cool them down.

The doorbell rang, and her eyes widened. Leo was early!

"Coming!" she yelled, toweling-drying her arms and jogging down the stairs. She threw open the front door to greet her big brother. "Leo!"

From the backyard, Sunny quacked frantically.

Leo chuckled and gave Vicki a quick hug. "Sounds like DuckTales back there wants to say hi."

"She always does."

Was that *gel* in his hair? Leo never paid much attention to how he looked, but today his hair was slicked back and he looked downright dashing in his well-fitted button-up.

Interesting.

Vicki closed the door and led Leo into the kitchen. He looked around and seemed to deflate a little. "Just us?" he said. "Mona's not here?"

Vicki bit back a grin. So *that* was why he'd taken a little more time with his appearance. "She couldn't come today. She got tied up waiting for the construction manager at the store. That rebuild has been a headache and a half."

"Oh, did that Mark guy not work out? The contractor?"

"No. And too bad. He was cute." She looked up at the clock. "Lunch is almost done. Cornbread will be out of the oven in fifteen minutes."

"Everything okay?" Leo asked after a long pause, studying her.

Vicki bustled to the stove and tasted the stew to check how it was coming along. Savory and delicious, just like the recipe had promised. "Aww, were you worried about me?"

Leo could read her better than anyone, and he always did feel like he needed to protect her. Plus, after what had happened with her last boyfriend, that big-brother instinct wasn't going away anytime soon. Not to mention that he was a cop *and* ex-military, she thought wryly. No, there would be no dissuading him from the idea that he needed to keep an eye on her.

Leo just shrugged, then peered through the half-open window at the fluffy, white duck. "Hey, Sunny," he said, tapping the glass pane. Sunny quacked.

"So, can I call you a crazy duck lady?" he asked with an amused grin.

Vicki rolled her eyes. "Very funny. As a matter of fact, I have *news!*" She sang the last word.

"Oh?"

A huge grin overtook her face. "We're in the Fall Festival! Mona and I snagged a booth!"

"Bam!" He gave her a high five. "That's amazing! As soon as you said that awful chair lady wasn't in charge anymore, I knew you'd get in. You'll outsell all the other vendors."

Vicki warmed at the compliment. "Well, it'll definitely be a lot of work to put it all together, but I'm excited about the challenge."

His nose wrinkled. "So, is that why it smells like a candy cane factory exploded in here? New product?"

"Oh! I was just putting the finishing touches on my energizing body scrub. Aunt Bee practically commanded me to bring samples to Coupon Clippers tomorrow. I tried some right before you got here."

He eyed her suspiciously.

"What are you laughing at?" She crossed her arms.

He held up his hands in surrender. "Not laughing! It's just . . . did you try it on your arms?"

"Yeah," she said. "Why?"

Leo pointed to her arms.

She looked down and gasped. They were bright red! *How . . .*

The spilled peppermint oil. She must have spilled a *lot*.

Her hand flew to her mouth, and she burst out laughing. "Guess I put a *little* too much peppermint oil in this batch."

"You think?" Leo asked. "Does it hurt?"

"It burned when I put it on, but I washed it off right away. Feels fine now."

His lips quirked in amused concern. "Seems like you could use some help."

That unexpected anxiety curled in her stomach again. Yes, she needed help. Because if she couldn't get this business off the ground, it was back to the soul-sucking days in the courtroom. But she turned on a cheery smile. "Would you like to sample the next batch?"

Leo scoffed. "No way. I can't go into work looking like I have second-degree burns. They'd stick me at a desk."

"Just tell them it was one of your crazy sister's concoctions," said Vicki with a grin.

"Like the soap that tinged my face green?"

"The guys understood that was my fault, right?" She affected an innocent face.

"Didn't stop them from calling me Grinch for the next two days.

No," he said, leaning back against the counter with his arms crossed. "I'm done being your guinea pig. Find someone else to torment."

"You know you'll help me out in a pinch."

"Yeah, right."

"That's what brothers are for!"

Leo laughed and reached out to mess up her hair like she was still twelve. He'd have her back no matter what, and they both knew it.

"All right," he said, "I'll help. Besides being your guinea pig or dumping out all your peppermint oil, what can I do?"

"Well, as you know, I learn from my mistakes, so . . ." She glanced at the clock again. "I think we have just enough time before the cornbread comes out. I'm going to whip up another batch of the energizing scrub. Could you grind up the fresh ginger root and astragalus?" She pointed to some dried herbs on the counter.

"Sure," said Leo, grabbing the herbs. He ground them with a mortar and pestle while Vicki mixed the oils, honey, and salt.

"Hope you didn't accidentally add peppermint to the cornbread," he quipped.

With a snort, Vicki said, "The cornbread came straight out of the box, as God intended. I only added milk, butter, eggs, and a little honey from my hives. But I made the stew from scratch, so that's what you should be worried about."

"I'm terrified to try it," he replied dryly. "So, Aunt Bee roped you into Coupon Clippers?"

Vicki reached into the bowl to test the consistency of the scrub, her nose twitching. "Yeah, maybe a month ago. You try telling Aunt Bee *no* when she puts her mind to something."

He laughed aloud. "I wouldn't dare."

Technically, Bee was Mona's aunt, but pretty much everyone called her Aunt Bee. The formidable woman always meant well, but her chief joys in life were clipping coupons and giving opinions. Lots and lots of opinions.

"She wouldn't take no for an answer, and said"—her voice took on an affectionate mimicry of Aunt Bee's dramatic warble—"*I know you need to start pinching pennies, especially after the fire.*"

"She didn't!" Leo cried, nearly dropping the pestle.

"She did," Vicki groaned, affecting wry horror so that Leo wouldn't see the panic rising in her throat. If this business didn't work out, she'd have to go back to being a lawyer.

That wouldn't be *so* bad, right?

But she couldn't even convince herself.

She took the herbs Leo had ground and started mixing them into the scrub with a vengeance. She'd just gotten so tired of seeing criminals go free. She wanted to live a quiet, happy life with her duck and her bees. That sounded like some real peace. Way better than working in the court system. The thought of going back to lawyering exhausted her all the way to her bones.

No. She wouldn't have to go back to being a lawyer. She'd *pinch pennies*, in Aunt Bee's words, until she made this business work.

She had to.

CHAPTER 3

*B*y the time Vicki and Leo finished the scrub, anticipation pulsed through her.

"Time to test it!" she cried, snatching the bowl from the counter.

"Hold on," said Leo, his face a picture of resignation. "You've already given yourself a sunburn. Let me try it on one of my arms."

"Are you sure, Grinch? You swore you were done being my guinea pig," Vicki teased.

Leo rolled his eyes. "Give me that," he said, taking the bowl out of Vicki's hands. He bounded up the steps, and by the time Vicki caught back up with him, he'd rubbed the scrub on the underside of his arm. They stood there and waited.

"How does it feel?" Vicki asked hesitantly. "Is there a tingling sensation?"

"Yeah, it tingles," said Leo. Then he started screaming, "It burns! It burns!"

Vicki gasped and dove for the sink. But Leo burst into uproarious laughter, and she whirled back around.

"You should have seen your face!" Leo crowed. "You actually turned pale."

Vicki's heartbeat slowed its gallop, but she couldn't help a grin. "That was *not* funny. Seriously, how does it feel?"

"It feels really good. It's definitely energizing."

"Good," said Vicki. "I wrote down the measurements, so I should be able to recreate it." She turned on the faucet so Leo could wash his arm, then she splashed him with cold water and bolted down the stairs.

"Now we're even!" she called.

And now she just needed to figure out how to sell those body scrubs . . . before she ran out of time.

Speaking of running out of time . . . Was she forgetting something?

At the bottom of the stairs, she stopped, sniffing. Peppermint still hung heavy in the air, but beneath it was another smell . . . an acrid smell that sent anxiety racing through her body.

Fire? Was the house on fire? Was her house going to burn down just like Mona's store?

She bolted to the kitchen, heart pounding, looking for the source of the flames. Nothing was on fire, but the burning smell was definitely coming from the oven.

"The cornbread!" she wailed.

She grabbed mitts and threw open the oven, coughing at the smoke. Then she pulled out the pan of cornbread and set it down on an open burner. The top was absolutely blackened. She closed the oven slowly, looking mournfully from the ruined cornbread to the clock and back again. She'd forgotten the cornbread in the oven, but it had only been in there an extra couple of minutes.

It might be dry, but it shouldn't be blackened!

She lurched toward the trash and pulled out the box with trembling fingers. "Oh no," she whispered. She'd cooked it at 450 degrees instead of 400. She smacked the box against her head, sending a soft poof of yellow-white powder into the air.

Footfalls behind her announced Leo's arrival. "Everything okay?" he asked, sounding alarmed.

She spun around. "It's fine," she said weakly, "if you weren't too set on having cornbread."

A smirk tugged at the edges of his lips. "I'm not too set on cornbread if you're not too set on salad."

"Wha—" Her attention snapped to the salad bowl on the counter. A certain white duck was beak-first in the romaine lettuce, looking entirely too satisfied with herself. "Sunny!" she shrieked. "How did you—"

But the answer presented itself immediately when she looked at the window she'd left half-open. "Sunny, did you come in for more blueberries and then decide to eat our salad?"

Leo nodded solemnly. "It appears that's exactly what happened. We can now refer this case to the district attorney."

With a long hiss through her teeth, Vicki said, "Well, we can eat stew? Or order takeout?"

Leo grabbed a spoon and sampled a bite of stew. "The stew will be fine," he declared. "Do you have biscuits or anything to go with it?"

"Mmm, I think I still have some frozen breadsticks we could heat up."

"Perfect."

Ten minutes later, they sat down to a cobbled-together meal of stew and breadsticks. *An odd pairing,* thought Vicki as she took her first bite. *But it works, somehow.*

"So," said Leo. "Grinding the herbs was actually kind of relaxing. Do you need any help getting your things ready to sell at the festival?"

"I was hoping you'd ask," said Vicki. "Would you be able to come over Sunday and help me make a few things?"

"Sure." Leo grabbed a breadstick. "Festival starts soon, doesn't it? I'm happy to help. Just don't make me a guinea pig too often." He stuck his tongue out at her.

She swatted in his direction. Were they still in grade school? But she couldn't keep the grin off her face. "Thank you! I'm so excited! Julia—the woman who hated us—was there today, too, and Kristen *still* let us book a booth."

"Oh?" He made a face. "I thought she wasn't running it this year."

With a shrug, Vicki said, "I guess she's deputy chair now, instead of chair? I'm not clear on the details, but it sounded like maybe her stepdad went around her back and got her demoted so she'd have more time to take care of her sick mom."

Leo chewed on his breadstick and raised his eyebrows. "Really? That's weird."

16

Vicki recounted the odd argument she'd seen and Kristen's explanation. "Some people are just very insistent on getting their own way, I guess."

"I guess," Leo said. "Oh, that reminds me of this absolutely bizarre case I just finished wrapping up at the station."

They spent the rest of dinner discussing Leo's most recent case. After he left, Vicki cleaned up the dishes and then went into the living room to watch TV. Not that she paid much attention to the show—it mostly hummed in the background as she jotted down ideas for the booth on a yellow legal pad. Finally, after a couple hours, she nodded, satisfied. Mona would have to approve the ideas, but Vicki was sure they'd have a great booth. Her phone dinged with an alert. Someone had placed an order on her online store! She skimmed the order. It was for her sampler package—a small batch of each of her honeys.

Might as well pack that up. She boxed up the honey and addressed it to the customer, then set it on the counter to take to the post office the next day.

After mixing up one more batch of the newly perfected energizing scrub and feeding Sunny, she decided to call it a night.

Just as she was turning out the light to go to bed, her phone rang. It was Leo again.

Vicki furrowed her eyebrows. *Why is he calling so late?* She answered.

"Did you hear what happened?" asked Leo.

Vicki sat up in bed, heart racing. "What's wrong? Are you okay? Is Mona okay?"

"Everyone *you* know is okay. Something happened at the park today. Julia's stepdad died under mysterious circumstances."

He died? I just saw him! "Mysterious circumstances? What happened?" asked Vicki, wide awake now.

"Someone pushed him off the bridge in the park—probably around two o'clock, we're guessing. There were signs of a struggle. We have Julia's brother in custody."

CHAPTER 4

*V*icki pulled on a pair of dark-wash jeans and a nice shirt, then squinted at her image in the mirror. She made a face, snatched a brush from the counter, and tugged it through her hair. Her mind wandered back to Julia and her family.

It was hard to wrap her mind around it. She'd seen the man alive less than twenty-four hours ago, and now he was dead. And Julia's brother was probably the killer? James had been a year ahead of Vicki in high school, and they'd had a couple of classes together her junior year—she'd even had a little bit of a crush on him that year. She wouldn't have thought him capable of such a thing.

What a tragic, awful mess.

"Can't be late," she muttered. She bolted downstairs and scooped two handfuls of samples into a grocery bag, along with a jar of her relaxing scrub for Mona.

Then she waved out the window. "Bye, Sunny!"

Sunny ducked her head beneath the surface of the makeshift pond. She'd probably found a tasty water bug.

Once in town, Vicki snagged a parking spot close to the library, grabbed her bag of samples, and jogged through the doors with five minutes to spare. Waving to the woman at the front desk, she strode toward the back meeting room, where the Coupon Clippers were jabbering happily with one another—Aunt Bee and Mona, of course, along with Sheldon Goldberg, Alana Morgan and her young daughter Tia, and Aunt Bee's twin sister, Aunt Cee. Vicki pulled up a chair between Aunt Bee and Mona.

"How are you?" asked Mona with a huge grin as Vicki sank into her seat.

"Good! Mostly. I still can't believe we're in the festival!"

Mona squealed.

She almost told Mona about the murder but decided against it. Getting into the festival was a huge accomplishment, and she didn't want to put a damper on it. Plus, Mona had been pretty stressed lately.

"Also," Vicki continued, "I think I've finalized the energizing body scrub. Leo helped me perfect it yesterday afternoon." She held up the plastic bag in triumph.

"Oh, Leo helped?" Mona asked, a faint blush coloring her cheeks.

"Sure did." Vicki suppressed a smile as she pulled out the jar of relaxing scrub and handed it to Mona. "He asked about you."

Mona's blush intensified. She grabbed the scrub, seeming almost desperate to change the subject. "Ooh, thanks! And I've got something for you!" She pulled a jar of jam out of her purse and passed it to Vicki.

"Yum!" Vicki exclaimed.

Across the room, Pepe the Chihuahua yipped, and twelve-year-old Tia Morgan scooped him up and murmured something soothing in his ear. Vicki smiled at the fidgety little dog. He was the unofficial mascot of the Coupon Clippers, and the librarians looked the other way as long as he wasn't too loud.

"Yep." Vicki turned back to Mona. "I had too much peppermint oil in one of the samples. I thought I'd burned my arms." She glanced down at the skin that had been angry and red the day before, but it had returned to normal.

Mona snorted.

"Leo helped me put together the next batch and was willing to try it out, and it worked really well. Now, if we could just find a place to sell these things, we'll be set," said Vicki. "Speaking of, how are the repairs on the store coming along?"

The heat kicked on with a gentle purr, and Pepe lifted his head, his eyes wide and his ears on alert. *Poor little thing always looks startled, doesn't he?*

"Not too good," Mona admitted. "The contractor never showed up."

"What? Why?" Mona had mentioned unreliable contractors, and they were way past their original projected reopening date of the Fourth of July, but Vicki hadn't realized it was *that* bad.

Mona shrugged, reached into Vicki's plastic bag, and pulled out a tiny tub of body scrub. "Beats me. Hard to find anyone reliable." She unscrewed the cap and inhaled the peppermint scent. "But it'll be okay, one way or another. We'll think of a way to get your products out into the market. I'm sure of it." She nudged Vicki and whispered, "I think Alana may want to talk to you about featuring your stuff on her blog soon!"

Vicki gasped. "That'd be amazing!"

Alana's blog, *Frugalicious*, got a hundred thousand views a day, or something ridiculous like that. When Alana had featured Mona's jam, Mona had completely sold out, and they'd spent days making more to fill all the orders. The money from that had kept Mona comfortable while the store was rebuilt.

"We'll figure out *something*," agreed Vicki, eyeing Alana. *I cannot go back to my old job.* The thought practically made her shiver, despite the pleasant heat wafting from the vents.

Beside Vicki, Aunt Bee coughed. "Can I have everyone's attention, please?"

The conversations quieted.

"Let the meeting begin," said Aunt Bee in a commanding voice. "Our last meeting was held here in the library." She paused to make sure Sheldon—the club's official secretary and one of its founding members—was taking notes.

He looked up at Aunt Bee and nodded.

Aunt Bee continued, "Sheldon, Vicki, Alana, and Tia were present."

Just then, Pepe barked. "Oh, yes, Pepe too. We went through last month's coupons to make sure none were expired, and then we swapped our newer coupons. Alana found a good coupon for buy-one-get-one-free toothpaste, and she shared that with Sheldon." She peered at Alana. "Did you find any others?"

"I did," said Alana. "I thought we could—"

"We'll discuss new business in a few minutes, dear," said Aunt Bee.

Alana closed her mouth and frowned, but Vicki suspected she wouldn't stay irritated for long. It was hard to stay mad at Aunt Bee.

"Now, where was I?" Aunt Bee warbled, studying her notes. "Ah! That's right. We traded coupons and agreed to meet at the library today. So, is there any new business?" Aunt Bee turned back to Alana.

But before Alana could get a word out, Aunt Cee spoke up. "I have some new business."

"Oh, really?" asked Aunt Bee, casting a quizzical look at her extravagant sister.

Aunt Cee wasn't really a member of the group, but she stopped by meetings sometimes to say hi. Today she was wearing a flamboyant ruby necklace and a chinchilla hat.

"Yes," cried Aunt Cee, tapping her colorful acrylic nails on the library desk. "When my boyfriend and I were dancing tango on our cruise, a talent agent spotted us. He wants us to fly out to Hollywood to be on a senior dance reality show. Can you believe it?"

Aunt Bee rolled her eyes. "Just remember who's paying for the flight and hotel." To the rest of the group, she added, "Not her boyfriend. That's for sure."

"Now, stop poking your nose into my business, Bee," said Aunt Cee. "You're just jealous because you never get to go anywhere."

Vicki sank deeper into her chair and glanced at Mona, who was staring at the gray carpet.

"That's not true." Aunt Bee pouted. "I can go wherever I want. I just *choose* to spend my money more frugally."

Aunt Cee scoffed. "*Spend* your money? The last time you spent your money was back in 1998. You got a new car. That was the last one you bought."

"Well, it still runs, doesn't it?" Aunt Bee crossed her arms.

"That's because you never take it anywhere," said Aunt Cee, adjusting her chinchilla hat.

Alana chuckled, and Aunt Bee turned bright red.

"Aunt Cee, I think the show is a great idea," said Vicki, interrupting their argument.

Aunt Cee beamed, and Aunt Bee huffed. Vicki was grasping for something conciliatory to smooth Aunt Bee's feathers when Alana saved her.

"I have some new business related to the club," said Alana quietly.

"What is your new business?" snapped Aunt Bee.

"Well"—Alana grinned, holding up a sheaf of clipped coupons —"Tandem Doughnuts has a buy-one-get-one-free coupon for doughnuts. I got enough for everyone."

"Wonderful!" Aunt Bee visibly brightened at the bargain.

Right! Free stuff. That would do the trick and make everyone happy. "I have free samples of my new body scrubs for everyone," called Vicki. "I have energizing scrubs, relaxing scrubs, and a scrub for dry skin."

"First rate!" exclaimed Sheldon as he jotted down Vicki's words.

Tia darted out of her chair, Pepe still tucked in her arms, and began rooting through the bag of samples. Vicki pulled out a relaxing scrub and passed it to Aunt Bee. *She could certainly use that one.*

As Vicki finished passing out scrubs, the members opened their coupon bags and pulled out the coupon sections from the newspapers that they'd been saving. They clipped what coupons they wanted and passed the sections around the circle. Vicki clipped a few coupons for groceries and another for a huge bag of Epsom salt she thought she could use in one of her products. Then she spotted one for Leo's favorite brand of flavored sparkling water and grabbed that too. After about twenty minutes, the coupons had dwindled, and Aunt Bee tucked the unclaimed ones in her bag and adjourned the meeting.

"Same time and place next week!" called Tia as everyone got up and put the chairs back in place against the wall.

Vicki tugged Mona's sleeve. "Hey, do you want to go for coffee or something?"

"Not today. I need to get back to the store and see if I can rustle up my contractor. Or literally any licensed electrician," said Mona with a loud groan.

"Go get him, girl." Vicki winked, crumpling the now-empty plastic bag and stuffing it in her purse.

She lingered for a moment, hoping to talk to Alana about *Frugalicious*, but Alana and Tia packed up Pepe and headed out the door right away. With a little sigh, she glanced at Aunt Bee, who was studiously pretending not to hear Aunt Cee's loud declarations that she had to get home to pack for her adventure.

Best to defuse that before they start sniping at each other again. She approached Aunt Bee. "Can I walk you to your car?"

"Thank you, dear," said Aunt Bee. "Could you hold my bag?"

Vicki nodded and reached for the bag, then almost dropped it and burst out laughing. "What do you have in here, Aunt Bee? The kitchen sink?"

"No, dear, just all of my savings from today," Aunt Bee exclaimed as they walked through the library doors into the crisp autumn air. "I went shopping before the meeting. You should see all the bargains I got."

Vicki glanced back at the library and caught a glimpse of a flyer for the Fall Festival in the window. Her thoughts flitted back to Julia's family. Could James really have killed his stepdad? Then again, it shouldn't surprise her. Not anymore. She, of all people, should know that just because a guy was funny and charming didn't mean he wasn't a killer.

She'd call Leo later and find out if they'd made any progress on the case. Maybe she'd poke around on it a little. After all, she'd worked in the DA's office right out of law school, so she'd been around her share of criminal cases.

But I didn't see any of the red flags about Alexander. And I was dating him!

She swallowed passed the lump in her throat and trudged toward her car. Maybe that was partly why she wanted to poke around on this case. Deep down, she was embarrassed that Alexander had pulled the wool over her eyes, and she craved some sweet-as-honey vindication.

But, no. Leo and the other detectives had this well in hand. She just needed to focus on staying afloat financially and getting her products ready for the festival.

Don't lose focus, Vicki.

CHAPTER 5

The next morning, Vicki took a full inventory of all her products and wrote out exactly how much she had and how much she thought she needed to stock the festival booth.

She grimaced at the numbers. This was all guesswork. How could she really predict how much she'd sell? What if the festival was a giant flop and they spent the money on the booth but didn't sell anything?

I'm just catastrophizing. She should probably go for a walk to clear her head before she harvested from her beehives. She felt jittery, and it was always best to harvest with a calm mind.

It was a pretty day, despite the chill in the air. Leaves crunched under her feet as she made her way down the street.

"Hey! Vicki!"

Vicki turned around and saw Alana walking Pepe. The Chihuahua was strutting along in a pumpkin sweater. *Alana probably knitted that for him—she's always so creative,* thought Vicki. *Maybe she could make something like that for Sunny.* Vicki snorted at the image of Sunny in a Christmas sweater.

Alana and Pepe caught up with Vicki, and Alana called, "I knocked on your door, but you weren't home. Thanks for the samples yesterday at Coupon Clippers!"

Pepe yipped, and Vicki bent over to scratch his head. "I was happy to," she said, smiling up at Alana.

Alana scuffed her shoe against the pavement. "They were really great. Tia and I loved them. I was wondering if you'd like me to feature them on *Frugalicious*. You could offer a discount to my readers? They really like BOGO deals."

Vicki squealed internally. "I'm flattered! Thank you so much!" Then she paused. She couldn't discount them that much or she'd only make about a dollar per scrub, but she didn't want to lose the opportunity. "I . . . think I need to keep my scrubs at full price until I can scale up production, so that it costs me less to make them—I don't make enough on each sale right now to do a buy-one-get-one. But I do have a good stock of some lip balms I made this summer! Do you think your readers would be interested? I could do a big discount for those."

"That'd be great!" said Alana. "I can send Tia over to photograph them for the blog." Her daughter Tia was an excellent photographer, and she took the pictures for Alana's blog as well as for the Coupon Clippers.

"Okay," said Vicki. "Call me soon, and we can set up a time. I have a bunch of flavors. I did sell off the vanilla, but I have lots of coconut and pineapple, and even some grape and orange. Since the store burned down, I wasn't able to sell nearly as many as I'd expected, and I'd rather not take the loss, so this is perfect. Thank you so much! You have no idea how much I appreciate it."

They chitchatted for another couple minutes until they reached Alana's house and said goodbye. Vicki kept walking, her mind churning over the possibilities. "Maybe the blog feature can jumpstart some online sales," she murmured. "I should make sure the scrubs are listed before the post goes live. Maybe some people will buy scrubs *and* half-priced lip balm. Oh goodness. How will I ever know how many scrubs I need to make?"

When she got home, she went into the closet and pulled out her beekeeper suit. The suit consisted of a long-sleeved shirt, long pants, gloves, boots, and a box-shaped hat with a mesh mask. It was awkward, but it kept stings to a minimum.

Before Vicki put on the large gloves, she grabbed her phone and shoved it in her pants pocket. She slid open the porch door and Sunny waddled over, quacking her little heart out. "Hey, Sunshine!" she cooed. "Should I put you inside so you don't follow me to the hives and get stung?"

Last time she'd harvested honey, Sunny had pooped all over her kitchen floor, but cleanup was a small price to pay to not have to worry about the little duck while the bees were grumpy. She picked up Sunny, set her on the kitchen floor, and slid the glass door shut.

Before she disturbed the bees, she lit a fire in a metallic bee smoker. The smoke would calm the bees and make honey harvesting that much easier. Vicki held up the smoker toward the hive, pulled the trigger to waft smoke, and waited for twenty seconds. Then she lifted the back cover and sent a few puffs of smoke straight inside.

Sure enough, after a few moments, the faint buzz within the hive seemed to settle just a little. She slid out the first layer of honeycomb, brushed some bees out of the way, and started to harvest the honeycomb.

So, I'll sell some of this at the festival. She put the comb in a bowl and replaced the frame, then pulled out the next section of honeycomb. *I'll need enough to make plenty of products to have in stock for the festival and online, in case that blog post really takes off like Mona's feature did. But how much?* She ended up with a nice bowl of honey and honeycomb, and some beeswax. *Good enough for now. We'll make everything we can with this, and then I'll harvest more.*

As she was sliding the last tray back into the hive, her phone rang. She started to reach into her pocket instinctively, then stopped and looked at her hands. Her gloves were sticky, and she couldn't take them off so close to the bees. She finished putting the frame into the hive. Her phone stopped ringing.

Surely they'd leave a message if it were anything important.

The phone rang again. Terrifying scenarios flashed through her head, each one more nonsensical than the last. What if Julia had gotten her kicked out of the festival after all? What if the festival warehouse had burned down and the whole thing was canceled? What if a giant swarm of hornets had taken up residence in the decorative scarecrows?

"Darn it," she muttered as she ran toward the house. She started pulling off her gloves. They weren't easy to get on and off, and the phone fell silent again.

Vicki sighed, tugged open the sliding glass door, and let Sunny run out into the yard. She set down the bowl of honeycomb and beeswax and pulled out her phone to check the messages.

"Just Leo," she said with a sigh of relief.

She listened to the voicemail. He was just letting her know he was running a few minutes late but that he was still coming to help her put together her products.

While she was listening to his message, a text came in from Kristen. *Hey Vicki,* it read, *could you come by the warehouse tomorrow to pick up your vendor packet? I'll be there all morning.*

Vicki grinned and broke into a disco dance. *Why, yes,* she thought. *I most certainly can.*

* * *

AT TEN O'CLOCK SHARP, VICKI PUSHED OPEN THE DOOR TO THE FESTIVAL warehouse.

"Kristen?" she called.

No one responded, but she could hear a woman talking loudly from somewhere in the building. It wasn't Kristen's voice. It almost sounded like . . .

She followed the voice to the left, through a door that led into a long hallway lit by harsh fluorescent lights.

Julia? No, surely not so soon after a family tragedy.

So it was a shock to see that it was, indeed, Julia sitting at a rickety desk in a cramped office, talking angrily on the phone. Vicki hesitated, torn between offering her condolences and leaving Julia alone.

"Well, we can't afford that!" Julia yelled, then hung up and threw the phone onto the pile of papers in front of her. Vicki swallowed and stepped into the doorframe.

"Hello," said Vicki, her voice halting. "I just wanted to stop in and offer my condolences. I'm so sorry to hear about your loss."

"Thank you," said Julia curtly. "If you're looking for Kristen's office, it's on the other side of the warehouse. Turn right when you reach the hall—looks just like this one. Hers is the third door."

Then, as if realizing Vicki had overheard part of her conversation, she added, "I was trying to get a lawyer for my brother. These lawyers either want a crazy-high fee or they're no good. It's been a frustrating morning."

"I understand," said Vicki, reluctantly sitting down in the padded chair across the desk from Julia. "This must be so hard for you. Do you . . . do you know what happened?"

Julia stared at the wall over Vicki's head. "My stepdad had gone to the park to sit by the bridge. He did that a lot. He liked sitting there alone, looking at the view. It was one of his favorite things to paint. He said, 'The light filters through the trees and casts some interesting shadows,' or some crap like that. As far as we know, there was a struggle, and someone pushed him off the bridge. The police think it was my brother, but James wouldn't kill anyone. He wouldn't hurt a fly."

"I'm so sorry," said Vicki. "I can't imagine if my brother were accused of something like that."

"And now my stepdad might get his wish after all. How ironic is that?" Julia's voice took on a bitter tone.

"What do you mean?" asked Vicki.

"Well, since he died, I might need to give up the festival."

"Why?" Vicki folded her hands in her lap.

Julia sighed and raked a hand through her uncharacteristically mussed hair. "I'm worried about my mom. She's been sick for a while now, and my stepdad's death and my brother going to jail might be too much for her to bear. Plus, my aunt—my mom's sister—is in town. She never liked my stepdad and would tell anyone who would listen that he was a mean person. You'd think she'd show some sympathy now that he's dead, but no. She's walking around either ignoring the fact that he's dead, or rejoicing in it. I can't stand her drama—I have too much else going on—but I sort of need to be there to be a buffer between Aunt Kelly and my mom."

"Oh no. That's horrible," said Vicki.

"I'm just trying to keep my mother calm and get my brother out of jail. It feels like everything is falling on my shoulders."

"Julia, I'm so sorry. That's quite a burden." Vicki leaned forward. "Let me know if there's anything I can do."

Julia looked at her, and her eyes flashed darkly. "I don't need your pity," she spat. "I can handle everything myself. In fact, if I were still in charge, I'd boot you out of the festival because your products are cheap!"

Vicki's budding sympathy withered. She shot to her feet, barely restraining the cruel retort that bubbled to her lips. Instead, she spun on her heel and stomped out of Julia's office and across the cavernous warehouse.

When she found the hall on the opposite side, she turned right. She reached the third door and rapped on the doorframe. Poking her head in, she saw Kristen sitting at a table, facing a window on the far side of the spacious office. Her back was toward Vicki.

"Hey, Kristen," called Vicki. "I came for the packet."

Kristen didn't move.

Vicki stopped. Something about Kristen's stillness seemed unnatural. Heart pounding, Vicki bolted toward the table, then gasped when she saw Kristen's face.

Kristen was dead.

CHAPTER 6

Kristen is dead. How can she be dead?

Vicki snapped her fingers in front of Kristen's face, just to be sure. "Kristen," she exclaimed. "Wake up! Please!"

But the pale, lifeless corpse just sat there, unmoving. Vicki's breaths came fast. She needed to call the police. To call Leo.

But one thought circled in her brain over and over again. *First Julia's stepdad. Now Kristen.*

Was it just a coincidence, or was there a killer on the loose?

Her ex-boyfriend's awful, handsome, smug face flashed in her mind. She hadn't seen the red flags. She'd forced Mona to expose him for the grasping, murderous villain he was. Well, now she was right in the middle of another investigation, and she wouldn't miss red flags this time.

But first, she had to call police. She regained her composure and called Leo directly.

"Hey, Vick. Can this wait? I've got a lot of paperwork," said Leo, his voice distant.

"Kristen's dead!" snapped Vicki.

All traces of distraction disappeared from Leo's tone. "Wait, dead? Start over. Who's Kristen?"

"Festival Kristen." Vicki choked out the details.

"Is anyone else in the building?" Leo demanded.

"Julia's in her office on the far side."

"Go there, and don't touch anything. I'll be there in three minutes, and the crime scene team will be right behind me."

They hung up, and Vicki bolted across the warehouse and into Julia's office.

"What do you want now?" Julia crossed her arms and leaned back in her chair, her face a picture of annoyance.

"It's Kristen," said Vicki, catching her breath.

"What's wrong?" asked Julia, looking worried.

"She's dead."

Julia paled. She got up from her desk and moved toward the door. Vicki stepped in the way and gently touched her arm.

"Get your hands off me!" Julia snapped.

"We have to wait here," said Vicki. "I called the police. They'll be here any minute. We're supposed to stay in your office and not touch anything."

"What happened? Where's Kristen?" demanded Julia, her whole body trembling.

"In her office," said Vicki. "Sitting at the table by the window. When I got closer, I realized she was dead."

A siren wailed in the distance. Vicki fell quiet, and Julia stumbled back a step and leaned against her desk as if she needed something solid to support her weight. Once they heard the front door bang open, Julia bolted past Vicki into the warehouse. Vicki followed, quickly catching sight of Leo and his new partner, Detective Ann Kimura.

Leo snapped his fingers at Vicki. "Come with me. Show me where the body is."

Detective Kimura led Julia outside. The door closed behind them just as Vicki and Leo reached the hall. Vicki pointed out the door to Leo and followed him into the office.

Leo snapped a few pictures of Kristen and the room, shaking his head grimly. "Tell me what happened."

Vicki had just finished explaining everything when she heard the door to the warehouse open again. "Over here!" called Leo. He stuck his head in the hallway and waved toward the crime scene team. "Victim's in here."

The officers streamed into the office and began processing the scene.

Then Leo turned to Vicki. "Come outside now." As they walked toward the door, he said, "I'll have someone else take your formal statement to keep things aboveboard. Please, just stay with them until I come back. Until we figure out what happened to Kristen, I want you to be careful."

They broke out into the bright sunshine, and Leo waved her toward another pair of cops who had just driven up. "Can you take her statement?" Leo called. Then he jogged back toward the warehouse while Vicki told Officer Williams exactly what she'd told Leo. She sat there and rested while a steady stream of very official-looking people walked in and out. A few minutes later, an ambulance approached. After about half an hour, the medical examiner and paramedics emerged from the warehouse with the body covered on a gurney. Vicki shivered.

Leo came back outside. "Too early to say for sure, but it looks like Kristen was probably poisoned," he murmured.

"What do you mean?" asked Vicki.

"Medical examiner sniffed the air and took a look at the coffee pot, which was still on and burnt. They told me the air smelled like garlic, which happens when arsenic is heated. They'll have to test the coffee pot and run a tox screen to know for sure," said Leo. "But with no visible wounds, it's our best theory."

"Oh, wow," whispered Vicki, feeling shaken. Leo gave her a bottle of water. Vicki sipped the water, and her nerves started calming.

She took a few deep breaths and looked at Leo. "I think I want to go home now. Is that okay?" she asked.

"Yeah. I don't think anyone has any additional questions for you. If they do, I'll let you know, and you can come down to the precinct. I'll call you later and see how you're doing," he said, compassion etched on his face. "I know this was a hard day."

"Thank you," said Vicki. She got up and realized her legs were quivering.

"Are you okay to drive?" asked Leo.

"Yes, I should be," Vicki reassured him. She was startled—more than startled. Shocked. Appalled. But she was also determined. This killer wouldn't get away with it.

Who could have done this to Kristen?

* * *

THE TERRIBLE THOUGHT CREPT UP ON VICKI AS SHE DROVE HOME. SHE shook it away, tightening her grip on the steering wheel. She hummed a song she didn't even like to give herself something to focus on.

Something to distract her from the fact that, since Kristen was dead, Julia would likely take over the festival.

And would probably take away their booth. She could see her business crashing and burning before her eyes.

A woman is dead. It's far too soon to worry about something as trivial as a festival. Even thinking about it felt gauche.

And yet, if she didn't think about the festival, she was going to be stuck picturing Kristen dead at the table.

Then her phone rang. *Aunt Bee.* Vicki hit *answer* on the dashboard, and Aunt Bee's voice filled the car.

"And how are you doing today, Vicki?" warbled Aunt Bee.

Vicki let out a long sigh. "I've had better days. Something's happened. Did I mention at Coupon Clippers that Mona and I got a booth at the Fall Festival?"

"Mona told me," said Aunt Bee, sounding almost alarmed now. "What is it, dear?"

"Kristen, the festival coordinator, has been murdered. I found the body a couple hours ago when I went to pick up the vendor packet."

"Murdered?" shrieked Aunt Bee. "Was she that woman who was so mean to you and sweet Mona?"

Vicki made a right-hand turn. "No, that was Julia, who's second-in-command this year."

"So, will Julia take over the festival? Will she kick you out of your booth?" gasped Aunt Bee.

Tears burned in Vicki's eyes, but she blinked them back. "I mean, I don't know. Maybe. Feels cruel to even think about it. Oh, but that's not all."

"Oh?"

"Julia's stepfather was killed two days ago."

"*Two* murders?" Aunt Bee cried.

"They think Julia's brother might have killed him, but Julia swears he wouldn't hurt anyone, and . . . I don't know. My gut says she's right."

"And you found the body today? Poor thing. You must be so shaken up," said Aunt Bee. "Where are you right now?"

"On my way home."

With a *tsk*, Aunt Bee said, "Nonsense. After the shock you've had, you must come over to my house for a cup of hot cider and a chance to gather your thoughts. I'll call Mona and have her come over too."

"Oh, that's really not—"

"I insist. I'll see you in fifteen minutes." Aunt Bee hung up.

Vicki blinked at the *call ended* message on her dashboard screen, then shrugged and pulled into a parking lot to turn around.

"Guess I'm going to Aunt Bee's," she said.

* * *

AUNT BEE LIVED WITH HER THREE CATS IN A SMALL BUT BEAUTIFUL house outside of town. She met Vicki at the door with a cup of steaming spiced apple cider. "Come into the kitchen, dear."

Vicki followed Aunt Bee through her living room, past dozens of family pictures on the wall and a handful of crocheted doilies on the coffee table. One of the cats, a shy tuxedo named Mildred, was curled on the sofa, while Minerva, the chubby brown tabby, followed Vicki into the kitchen, trilling for attention. She didn't see Merlin, the white kitten with black spots, which almost certainly meant he was napping or getting into something.

Vicki sat at the kitchen table, and Minerva jumped into her lap. Vicki stroked the tabby's chin and rubbed her ears, and was rewarded with a throaty purr.

Aunt Bee sat across from her, sympathy shining in her gaze. "You can relax here. Let it all out. You've had a hard day."

Wrapping her free hand around the hot mug, Vicki asked in a tremulous voice, "Is Mona coming?"

Aunt Bee nodded solemnly. "She'll be here in just a couple of minutes."

"Did you tell her what happened?"

"No," said Aunt Bee, "but I did tell her that you'd had a terrible day and needed your best friend."

Aunt Bee was always meddling and always giving advice, but today, Vicki wholeheartedly appreciated it.

"Thank you, Aunt Bee," she murmured. "That was thoughtful."

"*Brrrt*," chirruped Minerva from her spot in Vicki's lap.

From the window, Vicki caught a flash of Mona's car in the driveway, and Aunt Bee grinned.

"Looks like Mona's here already," Aunt Bee declared. "Excellent timing, both of you."

She bustled to the door to welcome Mona in, and moments later, Mona thundered into the kitchen and wrapped Vicki in a big hug. Minerva jumped off Vicki's lap to wind around Mona's legs.

"Are you alright?" Mona asked breathlessly. "Aunt Bee said—"

"I'm fine," said Vicki firmly. "It's just been . . . a shocking day."

Mona pulled back, a thousand questions in her gaze, then sat in the chair next to Vicki just as Aunt Bee produced a cup of cider for her.

"So, I guess I should start from the beginning," said Vicki. "The day we were accepted into the festival, I saw Julia arguing with her stepdad, and an hour later, he winds up dead. Pushed off a bridge. They've arrested Julia's brother for the killing."

Mona's hand flew to her mouth, and she blinked several times. "Wait, Julia's brother? Didn't we go to high school with him?"

"Yeah, his name's James," said Vicki.

Mona nodded. "I had some classes with him."

"Me too," Vicki said. "It gets worse. Today, I went by the warehouse today to pick up some paperwork. Julia was there. When I looked for Kristen, I found her...dead."

Mona shrieked, her hand flying to her mouth. "Oh, that's horrible! Are you okay?"

"I . . . I don't know. It's not like I really knew her, but it was so shocking to find a body like that. Leo thinks she was poisoned."

"Another murder?" Mona's eyes widened.

Aunt Bee nodded in grim agreement. "Two murders in a town like Magnolia Falls isn't a coincidence, I don't think."

"Also"—Vicki took a deep breath—"because this might impact your business, you deserve to know that right before I found Kristen, Julia and I had words. I went to offer my condolences about her stepdad and caught her on the phone saying she couldn't afford a good lawyer for her brother. She was mad I was there, and she said that if she were running the festival, we wouldn't be in it."

"Typical Julia." Mona rolled her eyes.

"But now that Kristen's dead, Julia might take over the festival, right? I hope I didn't mess up our booth by accidentally antagonizing her."

Mona looked as defeated as Vicki felt. "That makes sense. But we don't know for sure, right? I mean, do we still get our products ready?"

"Of course you do!" cried Aunt Bee.

Vicki slumped backward, and Minerva jumped back up into her lap and head-butted her hand. She scratched the side of the cat's chin and said, "I think we have to. She might not be able to replace us at the last minute. And maybe she won't even take over running the thing. She's worried about her mom and brother."

"Wow," Mona murmured. "You really have had quite a day, haven't you?"

"So," Aunt Bee said, "what are you going to do about it?"

"What?" Vicki's mind raced. "What do you mean?"

"Well," said Aunt Bee, "it seems as if there's a mystery to be solved."

Vicki snapped to attention. "Yes," she said slowly. "As a matter of fact, I was thinking about that. Thinking that I might want to look into the case."

Mona gasped. "Are you sure? I mean, after everything that happened a few months ago . . ."

Vicki held up her hands. "It's *because* of everything that happened a few months ago. Mona, I'm . . . I'm embarrassed that you recognized that Alexander was bad news, and I was swept up in the romance. This might be my chance to vindicate myself, plus save our spot in the festival, plus do some good in the world by keeping an innocent man from going to jail."

"*Brrrrt*," trilled Minerva, evidently disgruntled that Vicki had stopped petting her. Vicki gave her neck rubs to console her.

Mona quirked an eyebrow, but seemed to be giving the matter serious thought. "That's a great idea, but how are you going to pull it off? I solved the mystery of the store fire because I was right in the middle of it; police were asking me questions, and I didn't have any other choice."

Vicki waved a hand. "I worked in the DA's office right out of law school, plus I've been watching Leo do his job for a while now. He talks about his cases with me, probably more than he should. So it's not like I'm going in blind." She paused. "Oh, but don't mention this to Leo! He'll figure it out eventually, but I know he'll try to stop me. He's so protective."

Aunt Bee said, "My lips are sealed!"

"What makes you so sure it isn't James?" asked Mona. "If you prove him guilty, Julia will hate us even more."

Vicki didn't have a good answer for that. "Just a gut instinct," she said finally. "If I'm wrong, I'm wrong. And, notwithstanding the incident with Alexander, my gut's right more often than not. Besides, I'll talk it out with you and Aunt Bee. Two heads are better than one, so three heads must be better still. The hard part will be getting Julia to talk to me for five minutes without spewing venom."

"Hmm." Aunt Bee tapped her hand on the table. "If three heads are better than one, then what about six heads?"

"What are you talking about?" asked Vicki, confused.

"The Coupon Clippers, of course," said Aunt Bee with a grin. "I'll call an evening meeting for tomorrow, and you'll invite Julia! Coupon clipping is a great way to deal with stress, especially if someone's worried about money. It gives one a sense of control in a world that so often feels very uncontrollable. It's the best kind of therapy, I think."

Mona and Vicki shared a wry look, and Mona rolled her eyes.

But Aunt Bee continued, undeterred, "It will be good for her. And perhaps we can coax some information out of her that will give you some leads."

CHAPTER 7

*V*icki's heart pounded as she pulled up to the library at ten minutes to seven the next evening. Aunt Bee had made sure that everyone would be there by saying that the club had a new member in urgent need of coupon therapy.

Aunt Bee's car was already in the parking lot, and Vicki caught a glimpse of Sheldon Goldberg pacing on the sidewalk by the library's automatic door, underneath a street light. She took a deep breath. It was probably best to meet Julia on the sidewalk outside the library, so she got out of her car and headed toward the door to join Sheldon. Halfway across the parking lot, she pulled her sweater more tightly around herself. It had been pleasantly cool during the day, but was downright chilly now that the sun had set.

"Hey, Sheldon!" she called as she approached.

"Vicki!" he replied. "Just the person I wanted to see!"

She quirked an eyebrow. Really? She and Sheldon got along fine, but they weren't really friends. What could he want to talk to her about?

"What's up?" she asked.

"I . . ." Sheldon paused, then swallowed nervously. "Well, I . . . I was thinking of opening up my own business," he blurted. "Since you're an entrepreneur . . ."

Whoa. Sheldon was a known penny-pincher. *What planted such an idea in his head?* But instead, she said, "Really? That sounds great. What kind of business?"

Sheldon coughed. "A roller skating rink."

"Well, that sounds like fun." *And it sounds nothing like Sheldon at all.*

"I've always wanted to open a rink. It's been a dream of mine since I was a little boy. I always loved skating, and I want the children of this town to have a place they can go and have fun."

He was right—there wasn't enough for kids to do in town. "That sounds like a great idea, and you're so good at saving that you surely have the start-up money."

Sheldon nodded but didn't say anything.

"I'm sure the kids will love it. We should go inside and let the others know the good news." Vicki started walking toward the door but realized Sheldon wasn't following her. She turned back around. He looked a bit pale.

"Please, don't do that," Sheldon begged.

"But why in heaven's name not?"

"They'll think it's frivolous," said Sheldon, turning almost green.

"I'm sure they won't," replied Vicki, confused by his reaction. "We don't have a roller rink here, so you won't have any competition. Plus, I bet Aunt Bee will jump all over this. She used to skate when she was young. She'll love the idea."

"It's not Aunt Bee I'm worried about." Sheldon swallowed, his Adam's apple bobbing. "It's Alana."

Vicki furrowed her brow. "Why would you be worried about what Alana thinks?"

"Can I tell you something else?" asked Sheldon.

"Sure," replied Vicki slowly, the truth dawning on her. Perhaps the business idea wasn't what Sheldon had most wanted to get off his chest. This was a matter of the heart.

"I'm falling in love with Alana," Sheldon blurted, his expression stricken. "She's one of the most beautiful women I know. I'm worried she might see this business venture as frivolous and I'd lose any chance with her. Could you please not tell anyone else about the skating rink yet?"

"Sure, Sheldon," said Vicki with a wink. "I can keep your secret. You'd make a cute couple."

Sheldon's ears reddened, and Vicki caught a glimpse of Julia in the parking lot. *She really came!*

"Oh!" she exclaimed. "Our new member is here."

Julia wound around the cars, and when she came into full view, a sour expression flashed across her face. But then it vanished, as if she'd had to remind herself to be nice.

Fair enough. I have to remind myself to be nice too.

When Vicki had called Julia earlier to invite her to the meeting, Julia had been angry at first. She'd snipped, "If you're calling about the festival, I haven't made any decisions yet about any changes. I was hoping to have one day to catch my breath. Of course you *would* call the day after Kristen's murder to ask."

Vicki had to bite her tongue to keep from saying something snarky. "Actually, I was calling to invite you to a meeting at seven. It has nothing to do with the festival. I thought you could use some time away from everything. It's Coupon Clippers. My friend Aunt Bee says clipping coupons is the best therapy."

Julia had seemed startled but warmed to the idea, eventually saying something about welcoming the chance to talk about anything that wasn't *her awful family* or *the stupid festival*. She'd agreed to come, but Vicki had been half-convinced that she'd stand them up.

But she was here.

Julia reached the sidewalk, seeming tentative and shy. "Thanks for asking me to come out. I feel like my head is spinning," she said finally.

"I thought it could be nice for you to just sit and do something fun. This group can be a hoot," said Vicki. "This is Sheldon Goldberg. Sheldon, this is Julia Hewitt."

Sheldon's eyes widened, and he seemed startled for just a moment, but he only said, "Lovely to meet you, Julia."

Vicki looped her arm through Julia's. "Come on. I'll introduce you to the rest of the group."

They walked into the library in an awkward silence. When they reached the meeting room, they found Aunt Bee already inside, chatting quietly with Alana. Tia sat a couple of chairs over with Pepe in her lap and her camera on the table in front of her. Pepe gave a little *yip* when Vicki smiled at him.

"That's Aunt Bee," said Vicki to Julia, motioning toward the matronly woman. "She really is my aunt, but *everyone* calls her Aunt Bee. Come on—I'll introduce you." Vicki led Julia into the room.

"Hey, Aunt Bee," said Vicki, giving her a hug. "This is Julia."

Aunt Bee shook Julia's hand and welcomed her to the meeting.

Then Vicki introduced Julia to Alana, Tia, and Pepe just as Mona rushed into the room.

Julia gave Mona a curt nod. "Mona."

Mona nodded back, less curtly. "Julia."

They found seats—Julia between Aunt Bee and Vicki—and Vicki blinked twice as she took in the scene. It was such a weird collision of worlds to see Julia there with the Coupon Clippers.

Vicki noticed that Sheldon ignored the open seat next to Alana and, instead, sat across the table from her. But he blushed when Alana smiled at him. Vicki hid a little grin. She hadn't noticed the tension between the two of them before.

"Okay, I'll call this meeting to order," said Aunt Bee, pressing her palms together. "Last meeting we discussed some savings, and Vicki handed out some samples. We then sorted through our coupons. Is there any new business?"

"Well, we have a visitor," said Vicki. "Julia agreed to come today. She's been having a difficult time, and I figured the meeting could help her get her mind off her problems."

Julia shifted in her seat and offered a shy wave.

"Hello, Julia," said the group.

Tia picked up Pepe's paw and helped him wave back at Julia. Mona gave a polite smile.

"Hi," said Julia. Tears glimmered in her eyes, and she wiped them away. She cleared her throat. "Whoa. Sorry. Don't mean to be a drag. Guess it's been a while since I've done something normal. Thanks for having me."

Aunt Bee smiled and laid her hand on Julia's. "You are always welcome here. Let us know if you need to talk about any of it."

Julia sniffled and blew her nose. "Thanks," she squeaked.

"Everyone ready to swap coupons?" asked Aunt Bee.

Tia let out a cheer, and the swapping began.

Aunt Bee passed her first sheaf to Julia, and Julia handed it straight to Vicki. But Vicki shook her head and handed it back.

"Look through it first," Vicki said. "See if there are any deals you're interested in."

"Oh, but I didn't bring any coupons to trade," said Julia. "I shouldn't take any of yours."

"Nonsense," said Aunt Bee. "Why, it's your very first meeting. You should leave with some coupons."

Julia's fingers rustled the paper as if she wasn't sure, but then Aunt Bee passed another stack to Vicki.

"See?" crowed Aunt Bee. "Plenty to go around."

A soft smile crept over Julia's face, and she riffled through the stack, looking for coupons.

At the sight of Julia's smile, an unexpected warmth filled Vicki. Though she didn't think she and Julia were ever likely to be *friends*, she was glad to see her relax and let go of her anxiety and grief, if only for a few moments.

After about half an hour, Julia stood. "I should get back home to my mom."

"Are you all right, dear?" asked Aunt Bee gently.

Julia's chin quivered, and she plopped back down in her seat. Everyone set down their coupons and waited in expectant silence.

"No," Julia said finally. She glanced at Vicki out of the corner of her eye, and then the story exploded out of her piece by piece—her mom's illness, her stepdad's outrageous expectations, the way he'd meddled with the festival and gotten her demoted.

"And those were just last week's problems," she choked out. "Someone pushed him off a bridge, and he's dead. The cops think it was my brother, but it wasn't. I know it wasn't. He wouldn't ever. My mom's heartbroken, and my Aunt Kelly just will not stop acting like she's pleased he's dead. And now the festival chair has wound up dead, too, and what are the odds that's a coincidence? What if it's my fault, somehow? It's not like we see a lot of murders here, and I'm the link between my stepdad and the festival chair, and—"

A sob choked off her words.

Aunt Bee pulled Julia into a hug and whispered, "There, there, dear. It's no one's fault but the killer's. Always remember that."

The rest of the room sat in subdued quiet until Julia's sobs subsided.

Then Julia stood again, wiping at her smudged mascara. "I really was a drag, huh?" she said with a wry laugh.

"Not at all," said Vicki, and she meant it.

"I really do need to go look after my mom," said Julia. "All this has been even harder on her, and I'm . . . worried about her."

Mona made a sympathetic noise, and Alana reached out and squeezed Julia's hand.

"Okay, dear. Thank you for coming today," said Aunt Bee. "We hope you'll join us next time."

"Would you like me to walk you to your car?" Vicki offered.

"That's okay," said Julia. "You can stay and keep on clipping."

After the door closed behind Julia, Vicki looked at the group. "So, what do you all think?"

"We're trying to solve the case," Aunt Bee added, beaming.

"I knew Julia's stepdad," said Sheldon.

Even though Vicki knew it shouldn't have been a surprise—it wasn't like they lived in a big city—she found herself floored. "How did you know him?"

His gaze grew distant. "We used to be neighbors. His first wife, Maria, was like a mother to me. If you'd like, I could arrange a meeting with Julia's stepsiblings. Would you like to come along with me when I talk to them? I can ask them about their father."

What a break! "Sure. What are they like?"

"Well"—his face looked like he'd just eaten something sour—"they were never nice to their mother, though they were always vying for their father's attention. They were basically brats."

Tia stifled a laugh. Always-proper Sheldon rarely used a word like *brat*.

Sheldon continued, "I was more like a son to their mother than Laurence was—Laurence is Julia's stepbrother."

Vicki nodded, her mind churning over these new details.

"I used to go over and spend time with Maria, to visit over hot cocoa or help her with chores around the house. She was a lovely woman. When she died, Frank was wrecked. He married Julia's mom a few years later. I mostly lost touch with him and his children after Maria died, though I did attend the wedding. Julia was a bridesmaid. I also went to Frank's uncle's funeral—he died maybe five years ago? I liked Frank's uncle very much, as well. He had no children and loved saying hello to the neighborhood kids. He gave me a silver dollar once. Although I don't think he liked his own great-niece and great-nephew very much. But like I said, they were . . . brats."

Aunt Bee squealed. "Yes, you must take Vicki to talk to them. See what you can find out. And Vicki, you must come by my house again soon so we can brainstorm some ideas about the case. I've always dreamed of helping solve a mystery!"

"Yes," Vicki said, tucking her coupons into her bag. "I'd very much like to meet Laurence and his sister. Perhaps they can shed light on who might have wanted their father dead."

She wanted to interview James, too, along with Julia's awful Aunt Kelly. Even though the police thought James was the culprit and Sheldon had nothing but negative things to say about Julia's stepsiblings, Vicki thought that Kelly seemed like the most promising lead. She'd clearly hated Frank.

But she'd listen to everyone's story and draw her own conclusions. Maybe she could get into the jail to meet with James tomorrow.

As uncomfortable as the idea made her, she couldn't rule Julia out as a suspect, either. She had a clear reason to hold a grudge against her stepdad, and maybe she was mad at Kristen for taking over as festival chair.

"I'll call you when I set the meeting with Laurence and Linda," said Sheldon.

"Thank you," said Vicki. She stood and gave a firm, determined nod. "I sure hope we can solve this case before anyone else gets hurt."

CHAPTER 8

The harsh buzz of the jail's automatic door sent a shiver up Vicki's spine. At least she'd gotten inside—Leo hadn't gotten wind of the fact that she'd called the jail and asked to meet with James Hewitt, murder suspect. He'd figure it out eventually and try to stop her, but she wanted to cover as much ground as she could before that happened.

"James?" she asked the handsome man sitting at a table in the visitor's area. Her heart fluttered as memories of their high school classes together flooded back over her. He'd always been a bit of a flirt, but . . .

"Well, hello gorgeous," said James. "You've grown up."

Vicki frowned. That was forward of him. *Guess he's still a bit of a flirt.* She stuck out her hand. "I'm Vicki."

"I'm sorry. I was just teasing," said James. He seemed sincere. "No time for fun in this place, and I've been going a little crazy. But I remember you—we met in Mrs. Walsh's fifth-period English class, right? No need to introduce yourself."

Vicki rolled her eyes and decided to play along. "Hello, handsome," she replied in what was supposed to be good humor, but it sounded more sensual than she'd intended. Her face warmed. Composing herself, she sat down across from James, who was now grinning at her.

"So, what can I do for you, Vicki? You weren't exactly someone I was expecting to see here."

She liked the way her name sounded coming out of his mouth just a *little* too much. *Slow your roll, girl. Remember to not get sucked in by a handsome face.*

She'd made that mistake before and wasn't about to do it again. She didn't *think* James was the killer, but she'd remain open to the possibility.

She waved her legal pad in the air. "I've gotten to know your sister a little over the past few days, and I want to get to the bottom of this. Tell me what happened from your perspective."

He sighed, raking a hand across his face. "I wish I knew. I didn't do it, but that's all I can really tell you. That, and that I'm still worried—jail's not good for the soul, in case you hadn't noticed." He glanced wryly around the large, colorless room. "But I guess I feel someone has it out for me. That I was intentionally framed. Everyone who knows me knows that I go to the park to jog. I didn't even know Frank was there until an officer was putting me in cuffs and reciting my rights."

"I understand your frustration," said Vicki. "And I believe you." *I think.* "I'm working on the case in a private capacity."

"Well, thank you for adding an extra set of eyes to the case. And what pretty eyes they are," said James with another flirty smile.

"I'm happy to help." Vicki felt sure she was blushing. "I was wondering if I could ask some more general questions to help me get some background on the case."

"Of course," said James. "What do you want to know?"

"How often do you jog in the park?"

"All the time," said James. "I usually try to get outside and jog once a day. It's part of my routine. I lift weights too."

Vicki decided to give him a taste of his own medicine. "I noticed," she said, grinning.

His cheeks flushed pink. So he hadn't expected her to flirt back.

Two can play that game. Besides, he wasn't just a murder suspect. They knew each other. Sort of.

She cleared her throat, reminded herself to stay as neutral as she could, and continued, "Can you tell me about your stepdad's money situation?"

"He was basically broke. He spent all his money caring for my mom. From what I understood, he'd practically wiped out his entire life savings on her medical bills. I think that's why he wanted so badly to sell some paintings at the Fall Festival. But I'm not sure Jules was aware just how much he needed the money—he was too proud to say it. But that was one reason he was concerned about her volunteering all the time. He knew someone had to support my mom. I helped them out when I could, but he was sort of old-school. Thought that should be the daughter's job. He was a good man, and he loved my mom dearly, but he was a little sexist when it came to that sort of thing. It drove him nuts that Jules wasn't much of a cook."

"Do your stepsiblings know there's no money?" Vicki jotted down notes on her legal pad.

James shrugged. "I'm not sure. Probably. They would sometimes say snide things to him about wasting all his money on his second wife . . . as though he were buying her purses instead of treatment. But they adored Frank. I think they were probably worried about him not having enough to retire on."

"Can you tell me about your Aunt Kelly? It seems like she wasn't Frank's biggest fan?"

He snorted. "You could say that. She's harmless, though. I'd bet my life on it."

He really wasn't giving her much to go on. She rubbed her temples.

"What about Kristen?" she asked. "Did anyone besides Julia know her? Is there a connection with anyone else in your family or among your father's friends, that you know of?"

He shook his head. "Jules was the only one who knew her well. They were close friends. Aunt Kelly knew about Kristen, but she'd never met her face-to-face. My mom and I had only met her a couple of times, but Jules talked about her a lot. They were pretty close. I don't think Laurence or Linda or Frank had ever met her."

"Oh, okay," said Vicki slowly. *That doesn't look good for Julia.* "This is a delicate question, but I have to ask, because I haven't unturned other links, and I have to follow every lead . . ."

He looked resigned, as if he knew what she was about to ask. "Of course."

"Do . . . you think Julia is capable of murdering someone?"

"Absolutely not," said James firmly. "Jules can be strong-willed and competitive at times, but she's not capable of murder. Like I said, she and Kristen were friends. And they go all the way back to college. It's not a new friendship, or anything. They were girlfriends, you know? Like, movie nights and shopping sprees. Jules was the one who found Kristen a job here after graduation."

"I understand," said Vicki. "I didn't mean to imply I thought she did it. But we don't have a lot of murders here, so the killings might be somehow connected."

James stared at the wall above Vicki's head. "I've given a lot of thought to that, actually. I can't prove anything, obviously. It's just a hunch, but . . . can I ask how Kristen was killed?"

Vicki pursed her lips and met his gaze. "Poison, last I heard."

"How was she poisoned?" His eyes were intense and earnest, and she caught a glimpse of the agony he'd been hiding under his flirty exterior.

"Working theory is arsenic."

"Okay, but in what? How did they get her?"

"Oh. The coffee pot at the warehouse."

James slammed his hand down on the table. "I knew it. Jules was the longtime coffee drinker. Kristen had only taken it up recently. What if Kristen wasn't the intended target? Maybe the perpetrator meant for Jules to drink that coffee. Maybe the murders *are* connected, and Kristen was just collateral damage." Fear shone in his blue eyes, and he whispered, "I don't want anything to happen to my sister."

Vicki paused for a moment. "Thank you. That's a helpful angle for me to chase down. But don't worry too much—I'm sure Julia has a lot of people looking out for her right now." Even as she said the words, she doubted them. Julia's brother was in jail, her mom was sick, her aunt was wrapped up in hating Frank, her stepdad and best friend were dead . . .

Does Julia have anyone looking out for her?

"You're welcome," said James, a soft smile returning to his face as he recovered himself.

Vicki looked into his deep-blue eyes. *If we weren't in the middle of an investigation . . .*

Warning bells rang in her head. Memories of Alexander. *Don't do this again,* she cautioned herself.

"Could you do something for me, please?" said James, reaching out and brushing Vicki's hand, then apparently thinking better of it and drawing back.

"What?"

"Could you please keep an eye on Jules? I'm worried that someone is trying to hurt my baby sister, and I can't help her from here."

"I'll do whatever I can," said Vicki. Her skin tingled where James's hand had touched hers. They exchanged a few more words, and then Vicki excused herself and left the jail. Her mind whirled on the information James had given her. She broke out into the breezy sunshine, ready to make a beeline to her car . . .

And then she saw Leo leaning up against her car door, staring daggers at her.

CHAPTER 9

"What the hell do you think you're doing here?" Leo demanded, blocking the driver's-side door.

Oops. Vicki searched for a tame explanation. "Visiting . . . a high school friend?" she said weakly.

He scoffed. "You were visiting James Hewitt. My friend at the jail texted me and asked if I knew you were here."

"Hey! I knew James in high school," she protested.

"Oh, yeah? How many times have you talked to him since high school?"

Vicki fell quiet.

"That's what I thought," he said. "So, would you care to amend your explanation? Because I'm pretty sure this detective has figured out the truth already."

He could read her even better than Mona could. "And . . . I thought I could help you by asking my old high school friend a few questions?" Her voice squeaked on the last word.

"You wanted to investigate the murders," he said flatly.

She shifted from foot to foot. "And . . . maybe I'd happen upon some answers in the course of asking questions."

"No, no, no," said Leo, waving his arms. "You absolutely, one hundred percent cannot be involved in this. Let the police do our jobs, and stay out of the way."

She shot him a scowl.

"Listen, I just want to keep you safe," he said, holding up his hands as if to calm her. "Investigating a murder isn't safe. Making body scrubs is safe. Stick to what you know."

"Stick to what I know?" she demanded. "I worked in the DA's office. I'm not some sweet little college coed anymore."

Leo gave a long sigh and said, "I'm sorry. That came off as dismissive. But we can't have civilians investigating cases, because eventually someone is going to get hurt and sue the department. You don't even have a PI license. How would it look if I gave my sister free rein to poke her nose in police business? How do you think it looks *now*?"

"You didn't give me free rein to do anything," she said, "but you can't control what I do, either. And for what it's worth, I think you might have the wrong guy in jail back there. I'm not convinced James did it."

His nostrils flared. "And your track record is so great where that's concerned."

Vicki sucked in a sharp breath. She'd have preferred it if he'd slapped her.

He immediately seemed to recognize he'd gone too far. He stepped toward her. "Vick, I'm sorry."

"We'll talk later," she said in a tight voice, stepping around him and yanking open her car door.

"Vick," he pleaded.

But she couldn't stay. Couldn't talk this out now. If she did, she was going to dissolve into tears in front of him. She slammed the car door and revved the engine, peeling out of the parking lot. Her eyes burned with unshed tears.

"Focus on the case," she whispered.

To distract herself, she clicked open the Bluetooth menu and said, "Call Mona."

"Calling Mona," a disembodied female voice intoned in response. The phone rang a few times, and then Mona answered.

"Hello," gasped Mona on the other end of the line, sounding short of breath.

"You okay?" asked Vicki. It wasn't like Mona to be out of breath.

"Just finished my jog," she managed between wheezes.

"Your what?"

"My jog. I'm doing my cooldown walk now."

Vicki turned up the heat in the car. "That's what I thought you said. Why are you jogging? Someone chasing you?" She was only half-joking. Mona didn't jog. It was practically a point of pride for her. *Because I don't hate myself,* Mona always said with a prim look whenever people asked why she wouldn't take up running.

Mona snorted. "No. I thought I might need to start exercising. Trying to rebuild the store has gotten stressful."

"That bad?" *Guess I'm not the only one having a crappy day.*

Mona's voice softened. "I can't sleep at night. I'm shaking at times. My doctor recommended I try exercise first, so I decided to go for a run."

Well, Vicki couldn't argue with that. She made a mental note to check on Mona more often. "How was it?"

"Awful," said Mona. "Reminded me of all the reasons I don't run."

"You don't hate yourself?"

This time, Mona gave a full-fledged laugh. "I think I'll stick to walking for the time being. Maybe I should pick up racquetball or something. But you called. What's up?"

"Just wondering where you were. I'd like to hang out today. But if you're too stressed and just need to focus on the store, I totally understand."

"I want to see you too!" cried Mona. "I do have to be at the store today to deal with contractors, but why don't you come too? I'll be there in about an hour. Oh, and Julia hasn't kicked us out of the festival yet, so I guess we still have our booth? We need to get our product line finalized. Let's plan some fall-themed flavors?"

"Yes!" exclaimed Vicki. "I was thinking about a cranberry body scrub."

"Perfect!" Then Mona's voice dropped to a conspiratorial whisper. "Any updates on the case?"

"I did interview James. It went pretty well, I think. I'll update you at the store."

"Oh, I'll invite Aunt Bee too," she said, her breaths finally sounding even. "I know she'd really like an update."

"It's a plan!" cried Vicki, shoving Leo's angry face to the back of her mind.

* * *

"I BROUGHT A PEN AND SOME PAPER SO WE CAN WRITE DOWN OUR IDEAS," called Aunt Bee as she bustled into the half-built-out store. "Maybe if we sort through everyone, we can come up with another clue."

Vicki grinned at Mona. Aunt Bee was so excited.

The store renovation was further along than Vicki had realized— all signs of the fire had been erased and the electricity was finally working, although the wiring was still exposed. She and Mona had taken seats at a little card table that Mona had set up as Command Central for managing her contractors—and now, it could be Command Central for cracking the case.

Aunt Bee sat down across from Vicki with a notepad bearing the Best Western logo. "Okay, so what do we know? Should we lay out the suspects first and then hear about your meeting at the jail?"

"Sure!" said Vicki.

"All right," warbled Aunt Bee. "Who are our best suspects?"

Vicki hesitated, Leo's words ringing in her head.

Your track record is so great where that's concerned.

She swallowed hard. "Well, Julia's brother, James, was in the park when the murder took place, which is obviously pretty suspicious. He's toward the top of the list for Frank's murder."

Mona shot Vicki a quizzical look. "Did you change your mind after talking with him?"

"I don't know that he did it," said Vicki, "but with that much circumstantial evidence, I want to approach it carefully and with an open mind."

Mona and Aunt Bee nodded approvingly, and Aunt Bee wrote down James's name.

"Okay, who else?" asked Aunt Bee, a gleam in her eyes.

"I'm wondering about Julia's aunt," said Vicki. "She apparently hated Frank."

"What's her name again?"

"Kelly," said Vicki and Mona in unison.

"Julia's mother's sister, I assume?"

"Yes." Vicki tapped her fingers on the card table.

Aunt Bee scrawled *Kelly, Julia's maternal aunt*, below James's name on the list.

"I don't want to make this too formal, of course," said Vicki. "I haven't even met all the suspects yet."

"What about Julia?" asked Aunt Bee.

Vicki's jaw dropped. The thought of Julia's involvement had occurred to her from the beginning, of course, but she was surprised Aunt Bee had asked the question after how well she'd connected with Julia at the meeting.

"Well, we can't rule anyone out yet," said Aunt Bee, raising an eyebrow. "And as Julia herself acknowledged, it's odd that there were two murders so close together, and that she knows both victims so well."

"You're not wrong." Vicki let out a heavy sigh. "Julia did get into a fight with Frank, but she wasn't in the park when he died. She was at the warehouse. But Julia did want her old job as chair of the festival back, and it was Frank who got her demoted. Now that Kristen's dead, Julia might get the job back. That puts her on our list, although James didn't think she was capable of it. Said she and Kristen were good friends."

"Well, of course her big brother wouldn't think any such thing," said Aunt Bee. "You know how protective big brothers can be."

Vicki's throat felt hot and tight. Yes, she sure did know.

Mona looked at her curiously. "What's wrong?" she mouthed.

But Vicki couldn't get the words out.

"What about Julia's stepsiblings?" asked Aunt Bee, evidently not noticing Vicki's sudden tension.

"I don't know much about them," said Vicki, her voice coming out a little strangled, "but I'd like to meet with them as soon as Sheldon gets back to me. James didn't seem to love them, but he said they adored Frank, which echoes what Sheldon said. Their names are Laurence and Linda."

Aunt Bee added them to the list below Julia.

"What about non-family members?" Vicki mused. "A rival painter, maybe? Or he could have been having a dispute with a neighbor."

"And, of course, it may have been random," said Aunt Bee, "which will make finding the killer very difficult."

But Vicki didn't think it was random. She quirked her lips.

Mona shook her head. "There's either a common thread here, or a serial killer on the loose, or we're looking at the mother of all coincidences. When was the last murder in Magnolia Falls?"

Vicki shot her a wry look.

Mona groaned and said, "Okay, besides the death when my store was burned down. The point is, we don't get killings often here. So, two murders so close together? I don't think it's a coincidence. And Frank was a middle-aged man pushed off a bridge, and Kristen was a thirty-something-year-old poisoned by coffee. That doesn't sound like any serial killer I've heard of. Don't serial killers usually have an MO? Like, similarities between the victims, or killing roughly the same way, or something?"

"Yes," said Aunt Bee grimly. "The most logical option is, indeed, that they were targeted for a reason, that there's a common thread."

"So," said Mona, "how'd it go at the jail? Did you learn anything interesting in your conversation with James?"

"Well . . ." Vicki was interrupted by the front door opening. She turned, expecting to see one of Mona's contractors, but instead, a woman dressed in medical scrubs stood frozen in the doorway.

Mona stood. "Can I help you?" she called politely.

"Oh," said the woman. "You're not open. I'm so sorry. I saw the sign for the store, and . . ."

"Don't worry about it!" Mona said with a smile. "There was a fire a few months ago, and we're in the middle of a rebuild, but we're going to be open soon!"

"You're the owner?" asked the woman.

"Yes, ma'am. Mona Reilly." She crossed over to shake the woman's hand.

"I'm Claire O'Rourke." She returned the handshake. "I'm from Pigeon Hollow."

Vicki nodded. Pigeon Hollow was another small town about forty minutes away.

Claire continued, "I stopped off in Magnolia Falls for lunch on my way home and noticed your store. Do you harvest your own honey, by any chance?"

"Oh," Mona said, gesturing back toward the card table. "I own the store, but jams are my specialty. Vicki here is our queen bee for all things honey."

Vicki stood. "I do harvest my own honey, yes. I have a backyard hive."

"Wonderful!" cried Claire. "Are you already selling your bee venom to anyone?"

Vicki squinted. Had she misheard? "Selling my . . . bee venom?"

"Oh, for bee-venom therapy," said Claire, as if it should be obvious.

Vicki looked at Mona, then at Aunt Bee. They both shrugged. "I'm sorry," said Vicki with a little laugh. "What's bee-venom therapy? I mean, I've been stung, of course, but it sure didn't feel like therapy."

"It's sort of like acupuncture," explained Claire, "but with honeybee venom, using stings in specific places on the body to help heal it. Bee venom has so many healing properties, and it's wonderful for a number of chronic conditions. I'd love to give it to more of my patients, but I'm having a hard time sourcing enough venom."

"Oh, what kind of chronic pain conditions?" Vicki asked.

"Quite a few. It can be very helpful for some kinds of arthritis. A lot of my patients have long-term Lyme disease that hasn't been helped by the more standard treatments, and I've seen people literally get their lives back."

"Whoa. That's amazing!" Then Vicki's eyes widened. "Wait, do you use actual bees?" She thought morosely of her hive of beloved bees. Stings were an inevitable part of working with a hive, but a sting meant a dead bee—and that always felt like a little bit of a tragedy to Vicki.

"Oh, goodness, no," said Claire. "Well, some apitherapists do, but I source venom directly from beekeepers and inject it into my patients with a needle. That way, I can control the amount of venom and reduce the risk of my patients having an adverse reaction. Plus, it seems more sustainable to me, because it doesn't kill any bees. I install venom-collection systems near honeybee hives."

"Venom-collection systems?" asked Vicki.

Claire nodded with a huge grin. "They're basically fabric-covered plates with an electrical wire that gives off a very, very small current. The bees land on the plate and are annoyed by the electricity—it doesn't hurt them, it just annoys them enough for them to sting. The fabric I use doesn't trap their stinger, so they just drip some venom onto the plate and then go about their day. I pay by the gram, but most of my beekeepers make several hundred dollars a month."

Several hundred dollars a month? Vicki's mouth went dry at the thought. That could be a huge boost to her business—*and* help people get their lives back. "Does it hurt the hives at all?"

"Not in the least. In fact, some of my beekeepers say their hives started producing more honey after they started collecting venom regularly."

Whoa! "I'll research it," Vicki said earnestly. "But I really am interested. Do you have a card?"

Claire produced a business card from the pocket of her scrubs and said, "Seriously, call me—I'd love to talk more about it with you."

She left, and Vicki was almost lightheaded as she returned to sit at the card table with Mona and Aunt Bee. "What do you guys think of that?" she asked.

Aunt Bee seemed to think on it. "It seems like a great idea to me, assuming that Claire was being upfront about all the details." With a little giggle, she added, "I wouldn't want to see any of my little namesakes hurt."

Aunt Bee had made the pun about the bees being her namesake at least a dozen times, and she was never any less amused by it. Vicki snorted at the pleased-as-punch look on Aunt Bee's face.

"Definitely do your research," added Mona, "but it sounds pretty cool. Any income stream is a good thing, right? Speaking of which, what's happening with your feature on Alana's blog?"

"Oh, Tia came by to take the photos yesterday morning," said Vicki. "She had a whole bin of autumn décor to pose the products with. Hopefully some of them turned out. I'm not sure when the feature is going live."

Mona glanced at her watch and shook a fist. "My gosh, where is that plumber? He was supposed to be here twenty minutes ago."

"So"—Aunt Bee waved her pad of paper in the air—"where were we? Oh! You were just about to tell us about your conversation at the jail."

Setting aside the question of bee-venom therapy, Vicki recounted the conversation with James in detail, explaining his perceptions of his aunt, his stepsiblings, and his sister, along with his account of what had happened and his fear that someone might have been targeting Julia. Then she added, "Leo caught me there, and we had a fight about me looking into the case."

Mona's ears pinked at the mention of Leo's name.

"Well," said Aunt Bee. "Can he force you to stop investigating?"

Vicki shook her head fiercely. "He can limit me somewhat—he can refuse to answer my questions, or keep me from visiting James again at the jail, but it's a free country, isn't it? He can't control whether I talk to Kelly or Laurence and Linda."

Mona chewed her lip. "Well, don't tell him I'm helping you," she pleaded.

"I won't." Vicki suppressed a grin. It was so clear that Mona and Leo were interested in each other—Mona had been crazy about him since *high school*—but they were both so darn shy about it. The timing hadn't worked out before—Leo had been stationed overseas for a while, and after he came back, at least one of them had usually been dating someone at any given time. But, right now, both of them were single.

Vicki might have to give them a little push one of these days.

"Hmm. Well," said Mona, seeming flustered as she fumbled to change the subject. "So . . . so, James didn't name anyone as being particularly suspicious?"

Aunt Bee squinted at her notes. "But it does seem significant that he always jogs in that park. If someone wanted to frame him, it'd be very easy to do."

"And he was in jail when Kristen was killed," added Vicki. "So it's possible he killed Frank, but he couldn't have killed Kristen."

"And Julia might have been able to kill Kristen, but she has an alibi for Frank's death," said Mona.

"But," Vicki said slowly, "we don't know about the aunt or the stepsiblings, whether they have alibis. It seems to me like Kelly is the best suspect right now. Laurence and Linda, by all accounts, were very close to their dad, and we know that Kelly hated Frank."

"Why would Kelly have wanted to kill Kristen, though?" asked Aunt Bee.

Vicki shrugged. "That's what we want to find out. Maybe she was angry about Kristen taking Julia's spot in the festival? Or maybe she thought Kristen knew something about Frank's death? Or maybe James was right, and the killer was really targeting Julia. It hasn't seemed like Julia is especially fond of her aunt. Maybe the feeling's mutual."

Mona raised her hand, a hopeful expression lighting up her face. "Let's offer to take some presents over to Julia's mom," she said. "Seems like the family could use some cheering up, and that'll give us a chance to get to know everyone a little and maybe ask some questions."

"Great idea," said Vicki. "Kelly should definitely be at the house with them. Julia said she's staying with them right now. Plus, I promised James I'd look out for Julia when I could, so if there's the slightest possibility that Kelly wants Julia dead . . ."

"We should talk with them as soon as possible," finished Mona.

Vicki composed a text message to Julia. *Hey, I've been thinking about you and your family. Let me know if there's anything I can do. Mona and I were thinking of bringing some little gifts to your mom?*

After a moment, Julia replied, *Oh. Thanks. That'd be fine. We're wide open tomorrow, I guess.*

Vicki rolled her eyes. Of course Julia would be curt. But, then again, it had been a traumatic week for her. It wasn't fair to expect her to be effusive.

The three of them batted around ideas for another half-hour—Mona briefly stepping out to give some instructions to a very tardy plumber—and then Vicki's phone buzzed. She checked it to see a text from Sheldon: *Downtown. Now.*

CHAPTER 10

*V*icki pursed her lips and drummed the edge of the card table. It was unlike Sheldon to text at all, let alone so cryptically. She stood. "I think I need to find Sheldon," she said, showing Aunt Bee and Mona the text.

"Do you think he's found a clue?" asked Aunt Bee hopefully.

"I can't imagine what else it could be," said Mona.

"Go!" Aunt Bee shooed Vicki toward the door. "And keep us posted!"

"I will," promised Vicki. She texted back, *Am downtown. Where are you?*

The reply came in seconds.

Tiger Forest Coffee Shop.

The coffee shop was walking distance from Jammin' Honey. Vicki hurried out the door and turned left. Down the street, a young couple was pushing a stroller, bundled up against the chill in the air. Vicki looked at the oak trees lining the sidewalk, their leaves mostly yellow but with shocks of red and burnt orange. She loved this time of year. It was like someone was using the earth as their own personal color palette.

Her phone rang, and Leo's name appeared on the caller ID. She sent it to voicemail. She'd talk to him . . . soon. But not right now.

The overwhelming scent of pumpkin spice hit her when she pushed open the coffee shop door, bells jangling above her head.

"Vicki!" someone called.

It was Sheldon. He was sitting at a back corner table with two people who looked like brother and sister. They were both tall, perhaps in their late thirties or early forties, with dark hair and red-rimmed eyes, as if they'd been crying. The man had on a suit, and the woman wore a black dress. Sheldon motioned Vicki over.

When she reached them, Sheldon stood and gave her a quick, awkward hug. "What a surprise!"

Vicki played along. He must have texted her so cryptically because he hadn't wanted the siblings to realize what he was doing.

"Vicki, I would like you to meet Laurence and Linda," said Sheldon. "Would you care to join us for some coffee?"

"I'd love to," said Vicki. *Now's my chance to get to know them.* "Let me just get my cappuccino ordered."

When she returned to the table, she stuck out her hand toward Linda. "I'm Vicki. It's lovely to meet you."

The siblings each shook her hand, and then Sheldon said, "Laurence and Linda are old friends. I ran into them outside the bank today. They're in town to deal with their father's estate."

"Oh," said Vicki softly. "I'm so sorry for your loss."

"Thank you," said Linda, sniffing. Laurence put his hand on his sister's arm, and Linda pulled out some tissues.

"So, you're a friend of Sheldon's?" Laurence asked Vicki.

"Yes, I've known him for a while now. We met at a coupon club."

Laurence chuckled and rolled his eyes. "Why doesn't that surprise me?"

"We've known Sheldon for most of our lives," added Linda.

"Oh!" Vicki said. "Your father must have been that poor man who was pushed off the bridge. It was the front-page story in the paper. Sheldon mentioned at our meeting yesterday that he knew him. I'm so sorry."

Linda gave a stiff nod.

"So," Sheldon said, "how long are you guys in town for? I didn't realize you'd moved."

Laurence shifted in his seat. "Not sure. It depends on how long things take. We need to be here for the reading of the will—not that there's much to be spoken for in Dad's estate. Dad wanted to be cremated, so we're not sure when any memorial will be. We'll head back to Denver once things are finished here."

A blonde barista set a steaming cappuccino in front of Vicki. She thanked the barista and took a long, slow sip, getting a mouthful of foam and cinnamon.

"Have you stopped by your father's house?" asked Sheldon.

Laurence sniffed. His nose wrinkled like he'd smelled something rotten. "We have no desire to go there."

"But surely his things are there?" said Sheldon. "Don't you need to go through them?"

"Yes, but so is Julia," spat Linda. "She and James never loved him." The last word disappeared into a choking sob.

"I always knew they would do something like this," Laurence muttered.

"Like what?" asked Sheldon innocently.

"Murder our father," he replied darkly.

Linda squeaked, and Laurence put his arm around her shoulder.

Vicki's hand flew to her mouth in what she hoped was a convincingly shocked expression. "Julia and James?"

"Dad's stepkids," muttered Laurence. "James was arrested for the murder, and I'm not surprised. Julia was probably in on it. They always thought they were better than us."

"How awful!" exclaimed Sheldon. "Why do you think they did it?"

Laurence stared at him and raised an eyebrow. "Well, the police did arrest James."

"No, no," said Sheldon, raising his hands. "I mean, what do you think their motive was?"

Vicki took another sip of her cappuccino and admired Sheldon's quick save.

With a mournful sniffle, Linda said, "Laurence says he's not surprised, but it's mystifying to me. Money, maybe? Dad was basically broke, but James and Julia might not have known that. He lost almost everything in a bad stock fund several years ago, and most of the rest has gone to pay for my stepmom's medical care. He was trying to make it as an artist, but that never really took off."

Laurence added, "Our stepmom is really sick, so we don't mind her getting what little money there is. But we need to stick around for the will to make sure we get some items of sentimental value—some knickknacks our mom gave him, the paintings . . ."

Linda managed a sad laugh. "Dad loved those paintings so much, and I never really understood it. But now that he's gone . . ."

Laurence squeezed her shoulder. "We just want to make sure we get the things Dad loved before that vulture Julia swoops in."

Vicki thought wryly that Julia would be happy to pack up the paintings for them and say good riddance, but she decided to risk a pointed question. "You know, there was another murder in the news recently. Very odd in a town like this. Is there anyone else—"

Laurence's phone rang, cutting Vicki off.

He glanced at the screen and stood. "That's the lawyer calling. Linda and I both need to be on this call. It was good to meet you, Vicki. Good to see you, Sheldon."

He and Linda practically ran out of the coffee shop, the jangling bell announcing their departure."

After a long pause, Sheldon asked, "What did you think overall?"

Vicki ran a finger around the edge of her mug. "They're quite upset, naturally. It had to be a shock to find out he was murdered."

"I agree," said Sheldon.

"But Laurence *was* awfully quick to point fingers at their stepsiblings," said Vicki. "Did James and Julia really ostracize them?"

"They did seem certain Julia and James did it," mused Sheldon. "Although they may just be angry. An arrest might make it seem definitive, like the police are sure."

"Very true." Vicki took another sip of foam.

"But, no, Laurence and Linda weren't ostracized. They chose not to show up for family functions. I called a couple mutual friends I trusted to be discreet and asked about family dynamics."

Vicki's mind spun with questions. "I'd guess they're telling the truth about the money thing. James said something similar."

"Yeah, to my knowledge, Frank wouldn't have had enough money to kill for," said Sheldon. "He never worked any jobs that would have paid that much."

"And they came into town after their father died?" asked Vicki.

"Yeah, I think so. So they were probably in Denver when he was killed."

Well, being in Denver is a pretty solid alibi.

Vicki's gut still said that James wasn't guilty. After all, he couldn't have killed Kristen, and Laurence and Linda didn't seem to have any solid ideas for a motive for James—just hints that the relationship between the stepsiblings had been tense and an insinuation about money that wasn't there.

She sighed. At least she'd meet Kelly tomorrow. That might be a more promising interview.

"Hmm. Feels like we're going in circles," she said slowly. "But I do still have a good lead to chase down." Then she winked at Sheldon and shifted to a brighter subject. "So, have you asked Alana out on a date yet?"

CHAPTER 11

On the way home, Vicki stopped by the grocery store and picked up some cranberries for the first of her new fall-themed scrubs. When she got home and flipped on the kitchen lights, one of them sparked to life brighter, then died, casting the kitchen in shadows. *Another thing to replace.* But for now, the remaining bulb gave off enough light to see by.

She boiled the cranberries, and a lovely smell filled the kitchen. After she finished making the scrub and eating most of her enchilada dinner, the doorbell rang. It was Leo.

"Come on!" She grabbed the bowl off the counter and carried it over to him. "Smell the new scrub!" The cool scent of cranberry and mint wafted out of the bowl.

Leo sniffed it and nodded. "Pretty nice. Have you tried it out?"

"Not yet," she said. "But the mint is really subtle. There's nothing that could burn you."

With a wry look, he said, "Only because I really owed you that apology." He scooped up a little bit of the scrub with his fingers. After a pause and another sniff, he rubbed it in circles on his left forearm. "How long do I leave this on?"

"Just a couple minutes," said Vicki. "Does it tingle?"

"A little bit."

"That's the mint," said Vicki. "But there really isn't very much."

"I like it." Leo nodded. "You should call this one *Happy Holidays*."

After a minute or two, he stood and washed it off in the kitchen sink, then ran his fingers over his forearm. "Nice and smooth," he said as he sat back down at the table. "Works great!"

He excused himself to use the restroom, and when he came back downstairs, he was frowning.

"What's wrong?" asked Vicki.

"Look at my arm," said Leo. "Come into better lighting." Vicki followed him up to the bathroom. His forearm was light pink. She tightened her lips but couldn't hide her smirk.

Or her snort.

"Not funny," said Leo.

At the horrified look on his face, Vicki's laugh grew to a howl. Served him right for doubting her. "You'll be okay," she managed between bursts of laughter. "Should . . . wash off in a day . . . or two."

"A day or two?" Leo demanded.

"At most," Vicki reassured him, her laughter settling into an amused grin. "Thank you for testing this one. Now I know I should add fewer cranberries, or at least skip the cranberry juice."

"You think?" Leo turned the sink back on and tried again to scrub the pink marks off his arm.

"At least it's autumn," offered Vicki.

"What does that have to do with anything?"

"You'll be wearing long sleeves. No one will notice."

"I'll notice," muttered Leo.

"I swear it'll disappear by tomorrow night or the next morning. I promise," said Vicki. "Now, stop scrubbing, or you'll irritate your skin and make it even pinker."

* * *

"WE COULD USE BRANCHES AND LEAVES AS DÉCOR!" EXCLAIMED MONA from her spot behind the wheel.

"I. Love. It!" cried Vicki.

Mona and Vicki were on their way to Julia's mom's house,

watching the autumn colors out the window and brainstorming their Fall Festival display.

"We could throw some small gourds in too," Vicki said, tapping her yellow legal pad. "I already picked up a couple of big, decorative ones."

"Ooh, yes."

Vicki added gourds to the list. "Oh, I almost forgot to tell you about my new body scrub!"

"What'd you make?" Mona asked.

Vicki told her the story about the much-too-pink cranberry scrub and Leo's pink arm.

Mona snorted. "I can just imagine the look on his face! So, what'd you do with that scrub?"

"I threw it out. But then I cut out all the cranberry juice and added some orange essential oil. That worked wonderfully."

Mona chuckled again. "Was he mad?"

When they reached Julia's house, they rang the bell, and Vicki eyed the weed-filled flowerbeds. An older woman answered the door. She resembled Julia in the eyes and mouth, but was softer somehow.

"You must be Vicki and Mona," she said, offering a handshake to each of them. "I'm Kelly, Julia's aunt. Come on in!" She ushered them inside. The entryway was narrow but well lit, with blush-pink walls and a pretty wood table with a white vase and fake roses.

Vicki and Mona shared a long look as they set their purses and coats on the entryway table. So this was the mysterious Aunt Kelly.

"Thank you so much for coming, and for being so kind to Julia in the midst of everything. It's all been so hard on her." Kelly led them into the kitchen and gestured to a dinged-up yellow table. "Why don't you set the basket there? Julia will be out in a moment; she's helping her mom with something."

Vicki set the basket on the table and murmured, "Thank you. I'm so sorry for your loss."

Kelly's lips twitched. "Wouldn't exactly call it *my* loss. Lord knows I never thought the man was good enough for my baby sister. But, then again," she said with a shrug, "I'm not sure anyone would be good enough for my baby sister."

A door opened, and Julia stalked into the room. "Oh. You're here," she said, glancing at Vicki and Mona.

Vicki waved at her. "How are you holding up?"

Julia shifted her weight from foot to foot. "Fine, I guess. This is Kelly, my aunt," she said. "Aunt Kelly, this is Vicki and Mona. Although I guess you've all just met."

"Would you like some coffee?" Kelly asked, her voice as sweet as Mona's strawberry jam. "I just brewed a pot."

"Thank you," said Vicki. "I'd love coffee."

"Me too," chimed in Mona. "I never turn that down!"

Kelly bustled to the coffee pot and poured two mugs, then brought them to Vicki and Mona. "Oh, I'll get the cookies too," she said.

"You don't have to do that," said Mona.

"I insist!" Kelly scurried out of the room.

Vicki glanced at Julia. "She seems very nice."

"Just don't get her started on my stepdad." Julia rolled her eyes, then gestured to the basket. "Thanks for bringing that by. Mom's really having a flare—it's an autoimmune thing. Treatments haven't been working very well, and it's worse when she's stressed. She's obviously been unbelievably stressed this week, so she can't come out to thank you herself, but she's grateful."

The doorbell rang.

Julia closed her eyes and let out a long, frustrated hiss through her teeth. "I'll be right back."

She swept out of the room just as Kelly returned with a plate of oatmeal cookies.

"Here you go, girls." Kelly set the plate on the table. Her eyes lit up as she took in the baskets. "Oh! Are those for the Fall Festival?"

"Well, they're gifts for Julia's mom," said Vicki. "But we will be selling all this stuff at the festival. Do you want to smell it?"

"Oh, I would," said Kelly. "But are there any fragrance oils or anything artificial in it? I'm quite sensitive to all that"

"Not in the least," said Mona. "It's one hundred percent natural. Vicki even harvests her own honey and grows her own herbs."

"Delightful!" cried Kelly. Vicki pulled out each of the scrub tins, and Mona opened two jars of jam. Kelly smelled the body scrub and tasted the jellies.

"These are wonderful. I especially like the cranberry-orange scrub." Then she glanced at Mona. "I'm not usually a jam person, but yours are quite good, my dear."

"Thank you," said Mona, beaming.

Vicki chuckled. "I guess that's where Julia gets her dislike of jam."

Kelly laughed. "Julia knows what she likes and what she doesn't. But I am just so proud of her. I love how she's done so much for her community with this festival. Frank could never see what she was capable of." She looked from side to side and lowered her voice. "He was a jerk sometimes. Julia was *meant* to run this festival. She just brightens up when she's involved with something like this. Her mom thinks so too. Her mom and I have always encouraged her to do what she's best at. We just wish we could see the fruits of her labor in person."

Vicki briefly wondered why Kelly couldn't go in person, but then angry voices from the entryway caught her attention. Julia was arguing with someone. Kelly's eyes flicked toward the hallway.

Before she lost her chance, Vicki said in a soft voice, "I don't want to get Julia's hopes up, but I'm an attorney—well, I've been taking a break from law, but I'm licensed—and I'd like to prove that James had nothing to do with Frank's death."

Kelly's eyes lit up. "Bless you, dear. You're absolutely right. James wouldn't have hurt Frank." Her face took on a more serious expression. "I only hope police will believe us eventually, and that he won't have to try to convince a jury of his innocence."

Vicki chose her words carefully. She needed to fish for information on Kelly's whereabouts the day of the murder, but didn't want to tip her off. "Were you here at the house the day Frank died? Do you remember anything unusual, or did you see James at all that day?"

Kelly shook her head. "I was at home and didn't see James. He doesn't live here, anyway. He has an apartment downtown."

"What about afterward?" Vicki asked. The voices in the entryway were growing louder—Julia's voice, along with the voices of a man and a woman that sounded vaguely familiar. She pressed on. "What about after Frank died, or the day of Kristen's death? Did you notice anything strange? I spoke to James, and he's concerned for Julia's safety. He wondered if perhaps Julia, not Kristen, might have been the target. So, anything you might have noticed near the house would be very helpful."

"Hmm," said Kelly slowly. "I was here that day—we didn't want to leave Rose alone so soon after Frank's death. But it's hard to say if anything was out of the ordinary, because everything's out of the ordinary after such a tragedy. I haven't seen anyone suspicious, if that's what you're asking."

The argument in the hall fell silent, and then Laurence and Linda strode into the kitchen, Julia trailing behind them. Vicki jumped, startled. They seemed just as surprised to see Vicki as she was to see them.

More so, no doubt, since during her prior meeting with them, she'd feigned no knowledge of what was going on.

"What are *you* doing here?" asked Laurence.

"Fall Festival business," snapped Julia before Vicki could reply.

An odd lie from Julia. Vicki filed it away to think about later.

"I don't know how you have time to be involved with that," Linda sniped, smoothing her dark skirt. "Especially after Dad's death. It's almost as if you're not upset. Maybe you did this, and James is taking the heat for it. Or maybe you were both in on it together."

Kelly's jaw dropped, and her face turned purple as she squeaked in rage. Even Vicki was shocked—she knew Linda and Laurence suspected Julia, but she hadn't expected such open hostility.

"Excuse me?" said Julia, blinking icily at Linda.

"I mean, I'd think you would be trying to get James out of jail, not worrying about some silly festival," said Laurence with an equally cold stare. "Not that he's getting out anytime soon."

Vicki cringed and looked at Mona, who looked like she wanted to sink through the floor to escape the awkward situation.

"Oh, thank you for your concern, but don't worry—he'll get out soon," said Julia. "You can count on that."

"Well, we came by for Dad's things," said Linda. It didn't seem like she was even trying to restrain her contempt.

Laurence moved toward the hall. "I want to go into his office and look through his papers."

Kelly shot to her feet. "The lawyer said you can't have anything until after the will is read. You know that. You received the same letter we did."

"Well, we just want to look and make sure Julia and James haven't taken anything," said Linda, sulking.

A vein pulsed in Kelly's forehead. "The nerve of—"

"No," said Julia firmly. "I don't want you upstairs disturbing my mom. She's gotten worse since Frank died."

"That's too bad," said Laurence, looking like he couldn't care less.

Julia didn't flinch. "Get out of here, or I'll call the police and have you arrested for trespassing."

"At least give us his briefcase," said Laurence. "I want to look through his personal papers before the will is read."

"We could leave if this is a bad time," whispered Mona.

"That's okay. We were just leaving." Laurence stared down Julia. "As soon as we get that briefcase."

Julia threw her hands in the air. "If I give it to you, you'll leave?"

"Gladly," Linda barked.

With a disgruntled noise in her throat, Julia headed out of the room, her footfalls heavy on the stairs. Vicki stared at the floor, and an awkward silence descended on the house.

"We'll wait in the entryway," muttered Laurence, and he and Linda left the kitchen.

Mona let out a sigh of relief and looked from Vicki to Kelly with wide eyes. Kelly was still visibly angry, and Mona reached out and gave her hand a comforting squeeze. A chill ran down Vicki's spine. Too bad she'd left her coat on the entryway table. She decided to run and get it, even if Laurence and Linda were out there.

When she stepped into the entryway, Laurence and Linda were standing right by her coat and purse, and they whirled toward her with startled expressions.

"Sorry," she whispered "Just getting my coat."

They moved aside, and she grabbed the coat, almost jarring the white vase on the table.

Just then, Julia swept in, holding out a briefcase. "Now, get out," she hissed.

Laurence snatched the briefcase and spun on his heel, Linda following after him. They left, slamming the front door. Vicki pulled on her coat and wordlessly followed Julia back into the kitchen. With a heavy sigh, Julia sank down into a chair at the table.

"I'm sorry you had to see that." She rubbed her temples.

"It's okay," murmured Vicki. "Families can be difficult. How is James holding up?"

"As well as can be expected," Julia replied. "I saw him this morning."

"He needs to be out of jail for the reading of the will," said Kelly sadly.

"Ah," said Vicki. This was her chance to feel out what Julia knew about Frank's money—or lack thereof. "When is that?"

"In a couple days," said Julia. "Well, Saturday. Laurence and Linda have plane tickets for Monday morning—and good riddance to them —so they pushed to get it done over the weekend."

"If it's not too bold to ask, are you and James expecting to inherit anything?"

Julia shook her head. "I don't think so. I mean, we wouldn't inherit anything directly. He might have left some money for Mom, but he wasn't exactly rich. Not even close. Mostly I want to make sure Laurence and Linda don't pull some trick to try to cut Mom out of the joint assets. She relies on that money. She's too sick to work."

There was another long pause.

"Well," said Mona. "We'll leave you alone. Pass on the gifts to your mom whenever she's up to it."

Julia glanced down at the basket. "Oh. There's a body scrub in here?" She squinted at the label. "There isn't any fragrance oil in this, is there?"

Vicki's eyes flicked to Kelly, and she said, "No, it's all natural."

Julia nodded. "Okay, great. I'll pass it along to her and see if she likes it. She's sick with chronic Lyme disease, and even when she's not in a relapse, it's like her whole system is on a hair trigger. She can't be around fragrance oils at all, and she's sensitive to a lot of artificial stuff."

Chronic Lyme? Vicki snapped to attention.

"Oh," said Mona, glancing at Kelly. "Do you have the same thing? Was that why you asked about it before you tried it out?"

Kelly nodded grimly. "Rose and I both picked up Lyme while living on a farm in Virginia as teenagers. We both got sick, but she was a lot worse off than me. She improved for a while, but she relapsed pretty hard a couple years ago. She's been through a number of treatments, but nothing is giving her lasting improvement."

Mona gasped. "Oh, how awful!"

Could bee-venom therapy help Rose? Vicky wondered. *Should she say something about it?*

But Vicky decided now wasn't the time. Likely, a lot of well-meaning acquaintances had suggested miracle cures. She'd see if an opportunity presented itself to bring it up naturally—after all, she'd have to interact with Julia quite a few times between now and the festival.

"Yes," said Kelly. "My health never fully recovered, and I still get quite ill for a few days if I'm around any mold or dust or anything that sets me off." She glanced sadly at Julia. "That's why I can't see Julia's hard work on the festival. The last couple years it was held in a barn, and this year it's in an old warehouse—full of environmental triggers."

Kelly can't go into the warehouse. That meant she couldn't have poisoned Kristen.

"Well, we'll take lots of pictures," said Mona, "and we'll send them to you, so you can see it at least in part."

Kelly put a hand to her chest. "Why, that's so very sweet of you. Thank you so much."

They said goodbye, and Julia walked them out.

When Mona and Vicki closed their car doors, Mona whistled. "That was something."

"Sure was," mused Vicki. "I definitely didn't expect there to be so much drama while we were there. I can't believe Laurence and Linda openly accused Julia."

"Her aunt seemed nice, at least." Mona clicked her seat belt into place.

"She did," said Vicki as they drove away. "Plus, if she was telling the truth about her health—and Julia seemed to believe her—there's no way she could have gone into the warehouse to poison Kristen."

"Gosh," said Mona. "If she's that sensitive to stuff, she definitely couldn't have handled the arsenic that killed Kristen."

"Good point. I wonder why Julia painted such an awful picture of her," said Vicki. She hesitated, then said, "Can you take me back home? I need to do another hive harvest."

"Well, don't get stung," said Mona with a chuckle.

Vicki laughed aloud. "Don't worry. I'm a professional."

"Unless you've decided to try out bee-venom therapy," quipped Mona. "Then I guess you can get stung. Do . . . do you think the bee-venom therapy might help Julia's mom?"

"I was wondering about that."

They rode in silence for a while, then Vicki's thoughts flickered back to the odd scene at Julia's house. "Laurence and Linda sure were pieces of work. They seemed all right when I met them before, but man, they hate Julia, and vice-versa."

"To be fair," quipped Mona, "Julia hates everyone."

CHAPTER 12

*V*icki squinted down at Sunny. "What am I going to do with you?" she asked. "I really can't keep putting you inside every time I play with the bees. You make a mess and poop on the kitchen floor."

Sunny flapped her wings, and Vicki just shook her head. "What would you think about me selling the bee venom to make people healthier?" she asked the duck.

Sunny offered no counterpoint. Vicki thought again of Rose and Kelly, and an idea struck her. She sat at the picnic table and called Claire O'Rourke.

"Hello?" said a woman's voice on the phone.

"Hi, is this Claire?" she asked.

"Yes, it is!"

"This is Vicki Lawson, from the Jammin' Honey in Magnolia Falls?"

"Oh, hey, Vicki! It's so good to hear from you!" Claire sounded genuinely enthused. "Is everything all right? I hope you haven't changed your mind."

"No, I'd still like to sell my bee venom to you, and you're welcome to place the collection system at your convenience. I was just thinking about a . . . friend who might benefit from bee-venom therapy. It's kind of expensive, isn't it?"

"It is," said Claire, the regret clear in her voice. "And insurance doesn't usually cover it."

"Well, I'd like to donate all the bee venom you collect in the first month to be used for treatments for people who are really sick and can't afford it."

Claire's voice brightened. "That's amazing! Often, people with these chronic conditions end up falling into financial troubles because the disease interferes with their ability to work like they used to, so an opportunity for sharply discounted treatments would be a huge blessing for them. I already know of two or three people who would benefit. And I can put your friend on the list.

"That sounds great! I don't know for sure if she'll take you up on it, but I'll let you know."

Vicki hung up and turned back to Sunny. "Well, guess I'm going to need to find out if Rose is interested. And I *still* need to figure out what to do with you when I'm harvesting honey." Then she snapped her fingers. "I have an idea!"

She went inside and got on her beekeeper suit, except for the gloves, which she carried. Then she got the smoker and a handful of blueberries and returned to the yard. She showed the blueberries to Sunny, and the little white duck quacked in frantic anticipation.

"Go get 'em!" Vicki cried, tossing the blueberries into the plastic wading pool. Sunny jumped into the water and dove for the first blueberry.

"That'll keep you busy and away from the beehives for a few minutes," Vicki murmured as she put on her gloves.

Vicki had just gotten the smoker ready when Sunny started quacking loudly. "What is it?" she called.

Sunny's quacks grew more frantic.

She shifted backward and glanced toward the duck just as someone bowled into her. Something hard and heavy glanced across her head. *Thunk!* Stars exploded in her field of vision, and she tumbled facedown in the grass. Pain. Dizziness. Nausea.

Then she heard the distinctive *click* of a safety being released on a gun.

Pure instinct kicked in. Vicki grappled for her attacker's legs, trying to throw them off-balance.

It worked.

The person fell straight into the hive, and the bees exploded from their home in a buzzing, roiling, infuriated mass. Vicki rolled over and scrambled backward, fixing her askew face mask.

The assailant ran off, convulsing and swatting their body, especially their left arm. Dizzy and dazed, Vicki only got a quick glance of the attacker's back. Not enough to identify them. She lurched to her feet, scooped Sunny out of the pond, and stumbled into the house. Mess or no mess, she wouldn't leave her duck to become victim to the swarm of bees. She dropped Sunny on the kitchen floor and made it to the front window just in time to see a nondescript silver sedan fly around the corner and out of sight.

Her heart pounding, she called Leo and Mona, then went out to shut her hive. The swarm of bees would find their way back home, but she didn't want to leave the heart of the hive exposed to predators. As she closed it up, a few remaining bees divebombed her, and even through her suit, she got two stings. She swore under her breath and beat it back to the house, slamming the glass door closed.

She sank to her knees, breathing hard, and pulled off her gloves. Gritting her teeth, she yanked the stingers out of her arm, then slumped back against the glass door.

A few minutes later, she heard a car pull up. Her front door burst open, and Leo ran in. He stopped dead in his tracks when he saw Vicki.

"Are you okay?" he demanded.

"Fine," Vicki managed through gritted teeth.

The door opened again, and Mona thundered in behind Leo. "Let me help you take off your suit," she said in a calm, reassuring voice. Vicki had been so scared she'd forgotten she was still wearing the suit.

"I'm okay," said Vicki, holding out her arm where the bee stings had provoked two angry red welts. "Just a bump on the head and a couple stings." Mona pulled the helmet off Vicki, and Leo held up his finger.

"Follow my hand with your eyes," he said. "I want to make sure you're all right."

When he was satisfied she wasn't in immediate danger, he said, "Tell me everything."

Vicki described what had happened as best as she could but quickly realized she had little usable information.

"Let me check your head," said Leo. "Where does it hurt?"

"In the back."

Leo gently prodded Vicki's scalp, and Vicki cringed.

"Youch!" she yelped.

"A little blood, but not too much," said Leo, "and a small lump. Mona, can you get the first aid kit from the bathroom upstairs?"

Mona bounded up the stairs without a word.

"Say the alphabet backward for me," Leo said.

Vicki snorted. "I don't think I could do that before bumping my head."

Leo made a face. "Try."

Vicki surprised herself and got to the letter *M* before Leo nodded. "How bad does your head hurt?"

"Throbbing," she said. "And the spot that got hit hurts pretty bad."

"Vision okay?"

She nodded, then grimaced as the movement sent stabbing pain ricocheting through her skull.

"Your pupils look all right. Do you feel nauseated at all? Any ringing in the ears? Confusion?"

"Nope, nope, and nope. Except I'm pretty darn confused about why someone attacked me."

Leo glared at her for a moment, then seemed to realize this wasn't the time and schooled his expression into something more sympathetic.

Mona emerged from the stairwell and handed the first aid kit to Leo.

He continued, "Let me bandage your head so the bleeding stops, and then we'll get you to the hospital."

Vicki groaned. "I'm not going to the hospital. I'll be there forever and pay them a thousand dollars to tell me to take it easy for a week."

Leo's lips tightened, but he nodded. "Well, I know you well enough to know that arguing is pointless. Keep the bandage on for a couple of days. It's not deep, but I don't want you getting an infection. Don't take a nap this afternoon, just in case, and have someone here with you through tomorrow."

"Fine." Vicki didn't really want to be alone anyway in case the attacker came back to finish the job.

"Let me get you an ice pack and some aspirin." Mona was already opening the freezer.

"Okay, thank you," said Vicki. "I really appreciate you guys coming so fast. I hope I didn't make you leave anything important."

"Nothing's as important as this," said Mona firmly.

Mona prepared an ice pack, and Leo got Vicki a glass of tea. Vicki swallowed the aspirin in one gulp, then sipped the tea slowly and held onto the ice pack with her free hand.

"Why don't you go lie down on the sofa, and I'll take a look outside," said Leo. "Are the bees away?"

"They should be calm by now," said Vicki. "Although they might be a little extra sensitive. The smoker is out there and ready to go if they act up. Could you extinguish it when you come back in?"

"Sure," said Leo. He went outside, and Mona helped Vicki to the sofa.

"Could you get me the calamine lotion?" asked Vicki. "It should be in the first aid kit."

Mona grabbed it and uncapped the bottle, and the thick odor of the calamine was almost overpowering. Vicki dabbed it on the stings to quell a bit of the itching.

"Can I call Aunt Bee to let her know what happened?" Mona asked. "She and I can take shifts keeping an eye on you."

"Sure."

Mona walked into the other room and made the phone call, and a few minutes later, Leo came back in.

"Not even a good footprint outside," he said. "And no useful information from the neighbors."

"They're mostly at work this time of day," said Vicki weakly. "It's a weekday."

"Yeah, only one of them even answered the door, and he didn't see anything," he grumbled.

"Well, if we hear about anyone with a lot of bee stings who drives a silver car, we have our perp," quipped Mona.

Leo nodded and knelt next to the couch. "Not a bad idea, actually. I'll let the hospital know what we're looking for, and maybe canvass the local internists and family practice doctors." Then that scowl overtook his face again. "Now, Vick, why would someone want to hurt you?"

"Maybe they didn't like my body scrub?" She stuck her tongue out at Leo. "It wasn't you, was it? I didn't mean to turn your arm cranberry pink."

Leo scowled. "This isn't funny. I assume you're still doing your amateur investigation of the murders."

"No," said Vicki.

Leo glared like he didn't believe her. "Come on, who are you looking into? This is serious, Vick."

"Okay, fine," she muttered. "I'm still investigating, but I'm basically out of leads. Everyone has an alibi for at least one of the murders. I really don't have any idea who would come after me."

Leo rubbed his temples. "And this is exactly why we can't have civilians investigate. You're done with this case, you hear me?"

"That's fair," she said distantly.

He seemed to relax a little. "I'm going to make sure this incident is on record and call for a black-and-white to keep watch outside your house for now. Is there anything else you need?"

"No, thank you," said Vicki.

"Please stay out of trouble. And stop poking around the case." He radioed for backup, and when the cop car pulled onto Vicki's street, he left, muttering, "Need to crack this darn case before she gets herself killed."

As soon as the door closed behind him, Mona squinted at Vicki. "You sure you know what you're doing?"

"Maybe it means we're getting close," said Vicki weakly. "But who could it possibly be? James is in jail. Julia, Laurence, and Linda all have an alibi for Frank's death. Kelly has an alibi for Kristen's death—and besides, Frank struggled with his attacker. It wasn't like he was taken totally by surprise and didn't have time to fight back. Kelly didn't seem like she'd be strong enough to push him off a bridge. Rose is too sick to have pulled off either murder."

"Maybe it's someone else." Mona shrugged and brushed a strand of hair off Vicki's face. "This isn't a huge town; surely there are other people who knew both of them. Who else might have had it out for both Frank and Kristen?"

"But if it's someone else, why did they come attack me? It doesn't make any sense unless someone feels threatened by my investigation."

An official-sounding knock at the door startled Vicki. She looked at Mona, wide-eyed. Mona grabbed the nearest solid object—a decorative gourd Vicki had bought for the festival—and crept toward the door. Then she looked through the peephole and laughed. "It's just Aunt Bee and that officer Leo sent."

She threw open the door and assured the officer that Aunt Bee was a friend, and then Aunt Bee bolted through the door and to Vicki's side.

"Are you all right, dear?" she wailed.

Vicki smiled at her. "Just fine. We're just being cautious."

Sunny had waddled in from the kitchen and nudged Aunt Bee in her ample bottom. Aunt Bee glanced down and then jumped away with a shriek. "What is he doing in the house?"

Vicki chuckled. She'd forgotten she'd brought Sunny inside. "Could you take *her* back out, please? I brought her in to keep her safe from the swarming bees."

Aunt Bee looked horrified at the idea of touching the duck, but Mona swooped in and scooped Sunny up. Sunny put her bill into Mona's elbow, and her orange feet paddled in a circle.

"She helped out today, you know," Vicki called. "I had a moment's warning about the attack because she started quacking. I moved right before they hit me over the head, and the butt of the gun kind of . . . glanced off the side, if that makes sense. That's probably why the blow just gave me a knot and a pounding headache and didn't knock me out."

Aunt Bee's face softened. "Well, then. I'll have to make a special snack for that duck. What does she like to eat?"

Vicki laughed aloud. "Pretty much anything, but she's rather partial to blueberries. There's a carton in the fridge."

Aunt Bee marched into the kitchen and then let loose a bloodcurdling shriek.

CHAPTER 13

*V*icki's heart raced. Why had Aunt Bee screamed? What was wrong? Was there an intruder in the backyard? In the house?

But the next moment, Aunt Bee bolted back into the living room, yelling, "The kitchen floor is covered in duck poop!"

Relief filled Vicki, and she leaned back against the pillow, trying to keep her laughter contained so it wouldn't agitate her throbbing head.

Mona snorted. "I'll take care of it." She grabbed a rag and filled a bucket with soapy water. After a few minutes, Vicki tuned their conversation out, returning her thoughts to the case.

One thing was certain: it was more urgent than ever to put this murderer behind bars. And if she *was* getting too close, it meant . . . what? Everyone had an alibi.

Unless . . .

What had Linda said to Julia? *Maybe you did this, and James is taking the heat for it. Or maybe you were both in on it together.*

Maybe you were both in on it together.

What if Vicki had been all wrong from the beginning, and James and Julia had *both* planned it? What if James had killed Frank, just as police had said, and Julia had killed Kristen? They each had an alibi for one murder but not the other.

Leo's words flooded back to her next. *We're working on a theory. I can't tell you the details, but I can tell you that you won't like it.*

Why wouldn't she like it, unless it implicated James, thereby proving her wrong? She felt sick to her stomach.

"But what's the motive?" she whispered.

Killing two people over drama about Julia's volunteer role in the Fall Festival seemed . . . extreme. Mona was right—Julia seemed to hate everyone. But surely there was a big gap between being spiny and abrasive and being a killer.

Then two more pieces clicked into place in her mind. She'd asked Kelly some questions about the murders, had told her that she was trying to prove James innocent. Kelly might have easily mentioned it to Julia. And Julia had been to visit James this morning, so he might have told her about Vicki's visit to the jail. James might have even told her that Vicki had asked if Julia might have killed Kristen.

Which all added up to one awful thought: Julia might have motive for the attack on Vicki. Did Julia think that Vicki suspected her of murder and was being nice as a way of setting a trap?

Mona and Aunt Bee wandered into the room, and Mona said, "The duck is back in her happy little pond, and the duck poop in the kitchen is all cleaned up!"

"Wonderful," murmured Vicki. "Can we talk about the case for a couple of minutes?"

"Of course," warbled Aunt Bee. "I was hoping you'd ask. We have to catch the killer before they come after you again!"

Aunt Bee took a seat in the recliner, and Mona sat on the floor between the two of them.

"So," said Vicki, holding a hand over her eyes. Goodness, her head was pounding. "Mona, have you caught Aunt Bee up on everything that happened when we were at Julia's?"

"Yes, she did," Aunt Bee declared before Mona could answer. "She explained it to me while we were getting the kitchen all fixed up."

"I'm at a bit of a loss," admitted Vicki, her hand still over her eyes. "Everyone seems to have an alibi for at least one murder."

"Hmm." Aunt Bee pursed her lips.

"I *was* thinking that," said Mona slowly.

"Do you think we should expand our suspect pool?" asked Aunt Bee. "What about vendors who wanted to sell their goods at the festival but were turned down by Kristen?"

"But then why go after Frank?" asked Vicki.

With a shrug, Mona added, "And why go after Vicki?" She hesitated. "Should we look more closely at everyone's alibis? Do we know for sure that Kelly would get sick if she went into the warehouse?"

"That's something to look into," said Vicki. "Aunt Bee, could you write that down?"

"Of course." Aunt Bee jotted down a note.

"But I have a hard time picturing her as a killer," said Mona. "What about Laurence or Linda? Do we know for sure that they were in Colorado when Frank was killed?"

"Let's follow up on that too." Vicki rubbed her temples.

Aunt Bee made a note of it.

"But what's their motive?" Vicki asked. "Yeah, they don't like James and Julia, and their behavior was bad at Julia's house, but they loved their dad an awful lot. If Aunt Bee were killed, would you be civil to the person you thought had murdered her?"

Aunt Bee quirked her lips, and Mona let out a low whistle.

"Well," said Mona, "when you say it like that . . ."

Vicki slowly sat up. "I think I'm going to try to walk around just a little. Don't worry—I'm just testing out how I'm feeling. I'm not going to do anything crazy." She crossed to the front window that overlooked the road and stared at the autumn leaves in thought. "What if James and Julia worked together?" she finally asked in a flat voice, giving voice to the fear that had taken root in her mind.

Mona sucked in a sharp breath. "That would account for the alibis. You don't think . . ."

"But for them, too, we have to ask: What's the motive?" murmured Vicki. "Frank was driving Julia crazy, interfering with her volunteer work, but it wasn't like he was interfering with her career or anything. It was a volunteer position. And why Kristen?"

Movement on the road caught her attention, and after a moment, she realized Alana was walking Pepe down the street, holding hands with a guy. Vicki blinked. Not just any guy. Alana was holding hands with Sheldon!

Vicki grinned at the sight. One or the other had finally made a move. *Good for them.*

But then James's face flashed in her mind, and an unexpected pang of jealousy twinged in her chest. It felt like a long time since she'd had a real, functioning relationship.

Oh no. Were her high school feelings for James coming back? The thought of seeing him sent a little thrill zipping through her chest. *Oh, no, no, no, no.*

Sheldon and Alana continued down the road until they were out of sight, and Vicki bit her lip. Seeing them had brought her insecurities roaring to the surface. She wanted a boyfriend. Longed for a solid relationship. Wanted to put that toxic mess with Alexander in her rearview and find happiness with someone.

But now she was starting to fall for *another* murder suspect. Was this her pattern now? Was she going to be one of those women who mailed love letters to imprisoned serial killers?

She turned around and looked at Mona and Aunt Bee. "I'll go talk to James again tomorrow," she said, her voice steady. "I want to see if I can learn anything from him—whether that's coming up with another angle or even catching him in a contradiction. Anything to guide what I do next."

Mona's eyes narrowed on Vicki in concern.

"So soon after your head injury?" asked Aunt Bee. "Do you think that's wise?"

After a long pause, Mona gave voice to Vicki's thoughts. "Well, it might not be ideal to go so soon after a head injury, but if someone's after Vicki, it's not safe to lie around and wait for them to come back, is it?"

CHAPTER 14

*V*icki groaned when the jailhouse door emitted its harsh buzz. Her head was still throbbing, but it seemed better than the day before. Besides, she was on a mission. She wasn't going to let a mild head injury stop her.

As soon as Aunt Bee left Vicki's house the day before, Mona had offered to cancel her appointment with a drywall contractor and come with Vicki to the jail, but Vicki had insisted she stay at the store.

"Are you sure?" Mona had asked. "What else is wrong? I know there's something. It's written all over your face."

But Vicki hadn't been able to tell her. Hadn't been able to admit to the tumult of feelings about her love life and her career and how closely they were tangled together.

"Hey," said James, abruptly pulling Vicki back into the present. Her breath caught in her throat at the sight of him sitting at the visiting table.

James's brown hair was ruffled and his eyes were tired, but he shot a dazzling smile at her. His pleased expression turned to a frown as she sat down. "What happened to your head?"

"Someone tried to kill me yesterday," Vicki said, brushing the fresh bandage.

"That's horrible. Who did that?" demanded James.

"We don't know yet."

"Man, I'm sorry, Vicki. What . . . happened? Can I ask that?"

She hesitated, feeling awkward sitting in front of him. Last time had been so much easier, because in their previous meeting, she'd been pretty sure he hadn't killed anyone. She'd been almost certain she was talking to an innocent man.

But now her guard was up.

She chose each word carefully. "I assume either the person who killed Frank or the person who killed Kristen."

James blinked three times, as if trying to process what Vicki was saying. "Wait . . . *either* the person who killed Frank or the person who killed Kristen? Are you . . . saying you think those are two different people?"

"I'm not sure," she said, hating how clipped her voice sounded. "I'm working on a few theories and trying to poke holes in some alibis. I thought I'd come here to ask you a few more questions."

"Sure. Of course." He leaned back in his chair, a troubled look on his face.

The door buzzed open, and a guard poked his head in. "Miss Lawson?"

Vicki turned her head to face him. "Yes?"

"I'm going to need you to come with me," he said.

She stared at him. Visiting hours weren't close to over. Then the realization hit her. This interference had Leo written all over it. "And why's that?" she asked sweetly.

"Request from the lead detective on the case," he said.

Bingo. Leo had found out she was here.

"I'm sorry," the guard continued, "but he didn't want you questioning the suspect."

"Questioning?" said Vicki innocently. "Oh, I'm so sorry—there's been a misunderstanding. I'm an attorney."

The guard squinted at her as if he didn't quite believe her.

"I hope you know that everyone in this country has the right to legal counsel when they're accused of a crime." She crossed her arms.

He opened his mouth but seemed to think better of whatever

question he was about to ask. Slowly, he nodded and withdrew from the room.

When the door closed, James said, "You're really an attorney? Or were you just saying that to buy time?"

Shifting in her chair, she said, "It's complicated. I mean, I really am a licensed attorney and a member of the bar. I'm not currently practicing. Got tired of it and wanted to try entrepreneurship. That's how I know Julia. My friend and I are vendors in the Fall Festival." Then she lowered her voice. "If the guard comes back, back me up. Tell him I'm one of your attorneys. I won't send you a bill, I promise. But he can't kick me out of here if I'm your lawyer, no matter what the lead detective on the case says."

He grinned. "Noted."

"Now," she said, "I'm having some trouble, because I think I'm on the tail of whoever did this, but everyone seems to have an alibi, and I don't have a clear idea of a motive."

His smile faded, and he tilted his head. "That . . . doesn't sound like you're on the tail of someone. No offense intended."

She chuckled, even though it made her head throb. "No offense taken." Why did his hair so darn charming when it was mussed like that? She gestured to the bandage on the side of her head. "But I don't think the killer snuck into my yard and whacked me over the head because they were mad I wasn't making any progress."

With a grimace, he replied, "Fair enough."

She decided to start out with a softball question. "I want to know a little more about Frank's family," she said. "What can you tell me about them?"

"Well, he didn't have much family to speak of anymore—just Laurence and Linda and my mom," said James. "His first wife, Maria, died years ago. His parents died when he was in his twenties, and he had no siblings."

Vicki's eyebrows knitted together. Sheldon had said something about another family member. A brother? No, an uncle, she thought.

"Was he in contact with an uncle?" she asked.

"Oh, his uncle did live with him for a while several years ago," he said. "But he passed away four or five years back." He smiled softly. "I didn't know him for very long, but even in that short amount of time, he made an impression. We all called him Uncle Jack. He had the best stories. He used to travel all over the world. If you believed him, he once danced with Princess Diana in Australia."

"Did he really?" Vicki asked with wide eyes.

James shrugged. "Who's to say? But I doubt it. He also said that a wolf once led him to a cache of diamonds buried near his cabin in Alaska and that the agent that James Bond was based on rescued him from pirates off the coast of Africa."

She chuckled, relaxing just a little. "Sounds like he really did have the best stories."

"That was Uncle Jack for ya," he said. "You'd believe anything while he was talking to you though, and you never really wanted to think too hard to sort out what was true and what wasn't."

Vicki returned to the task at hand. "So, no other living family . . . What can you tell me about your mom's health? How'd she get sick?"

"Lyme disease," he said sadly. "Mom and Aunt Kelly both. Aunt Kelly's mostly better now—she thinks she's recovered from the Lyme, but the toll it took on her body means that her health can be touch-and-go. But Mom's been in a full relapse and has debilitating symptoms most days."

Well, that certainly buttressed the idea that Kelly couldn't have done it. Which made it increasingly likely that James and Julia were in on it together. Vicki felt sick to her stomach. What if Julia had poisoned Kristen to take the heat off James? To confuse police and throw them off the trail?

It was a better motive than anything else she'd come up with.

But she still hoped they were innocent.

"Unrelated, do you know what all treatments your mom has tried for the Lyme?"

Shaking his head, he said, "Just about everything. Antibiotics, of course. Long-term antibiotics worked for Aunt Kelly. Stem-cell therapy—not sure how she and Frank ever afforded that. I offered to help pay for it, but she said they had it covered. Um . . . some herbal stuff. Colloidal silver, I think?"

"Did she ever try bee-venom therapy?"

His face crinkled. "No, I think I'd remember that one. What's that?"

"Just something I heard about recently. I was just curious."

"Well, if there's any possibility it might help, she'd be interested to try it, as long as she can find the money," he said. "When you're that desperate for a cure, you'll try anything."

Good to know. She studied him with a neutral expression and stood. "I think that's all for now. Thank you for your time."

"Wait! Could you do something for me, please?"

"Hmm?"

Since you're my attorney, and all," he said with a wink.

Vicki paused. "What?"

"Could you please go to the reading of Frank's will tomorrow, as my representative? I'm still worried about Jules's safety, and I'd feel better if I knew someone was there keeping a sharp eye out for anything strange."

She hesitated. Even though her suspicions of James were growing, it was a rock-solid, unimpeachable reason to attend the reading of the will, which would give her an opportunity to dig around just a little more.

"Sure," she said, hoping with every fiber of her being that she wouldn't regret it.

CHAPTER 15

When Vicki left the jail, she clutched her jacket more tightly around her, then checked her phone and found a text from Leo. *Hey,* it read, *how's your head?*

She quirked her lips. Leo had known she was at the jail and had sent that guard in to try to pull her out. But she decided to ignore that. *Pretty good,* she replied. *Still have a little bit of a headache, but that's to be expected. No other symptoms.*

As she walked out to her car, her phone buzzed again. *Can we get coffee?* Leo asked. *Meet me at the station?*

Vicki rubbed her temples with her free hand. She didn't have the energy for another fight. She replied, *Only if talk of the case is 100% off-limits.*

The phone buzzed. *No promises, kid. But plz come. I promise to be nice.*

She let out a long sigh and typed, *On my way.*

The station was only a block and a half from the jail, but after yesterday's attack, she decided to drive rather than walk. Strains of the Bee Gees streamed from the radio, and she hummed under her breath as her car headed down the street.

She parked and reached up to rub the knot on her head. This would be fine. This would all be fine.

But would it be? Why did it feel like her life was falling apart?

95

Maybe it was ridiculous, but it felt like both her professional and her personal lives hinged on whatever happened over the next few days.

Shaking her head, she texted Leo, *Here.* She turned up the radio and waited.

Thirty seconds later, another car turned into the parking lot, and she startled when she realized Laurence was driving.

What's he doing here?

She put the phone down, and Laurence parked his car—a black Lexus, not a silver sedan, she noted with disappointment—and headed into the police station carrying a sheaf of papers. Vicki took a deep breath, then turned off her car and followed. She caught up with him just as he reached the door.

"Laurence?" she said, pretending to be surprised to see him.

He whipped toward her, and his face crinkled like he'd tasted something sour. "You *again?*" he demanded. "What are you doing here? Are you following me?"

"On the contrary," Vicki said, crossing her arms. "I should ask if you're following *me*. You showed up when I was at Rose's house, and I arrived here at the station before you did. I'm meeting someone, if you must know."

"Well, whatever it is you're doing"—he waved the papers in her face—"James is definitely guilty, and Julia was probably in on it too."

"Oh, well it's nothing to me either way," Vicki said, affecting a casual tone. "I don't know them well. I found out after we met at the coffee shop with Sheldon that you were talking about the same Julia who's deputy chair of the Fall Festival—I'm a vendor there." Then she chuckled. "But I can't deny being curious. This isn't a town that sees a lot of excitement. What makes you think James and Julia did it?"

He eyed her suspiciously but didn't seem eager to keep his cards close to his chest. "I found this in Dad's briefcase." He waved the sheaf of papers again. "It's a life insurance policy. I knew he had one, but I wasn't sure if it had expired yet or not. But it's still valid for one more year. Eight months ago, the beneficiaries on it were changed. It used to be for Linda and me, but Frank changed it to give the money jointly to his wife, James, and Julia."

Vicki inhaled sharply. "Whoa," she said, trying to look like this wasn't a punch in the stomach. "That's certainly something, isn't it?"

Motive. It was cold, hard motive. There *was* money after all—in a life insurance policy. Julia and her whole family stood to benefit if Frank died before the policy expired. Vicki caught a glimpse of the first page. It wasn't a huge policy—just fifty thousand dollars—but it was certainly a lot more than Frank was making from selling his paintings.

Had they needed the money for treatments for Rose? Had they really been that desperate? James's words at the jail took on a new significance. *If there's any possibility it might help, she'd be interested to try it, as long as she can find the money. When you're that desperate for a cure, you'll try anything.*

Laurence stalked toward the officer at the front desk and snapped, "I need to speak to someone working on the Frank Young murder."

Vicki drifted to one of the chairs in the lobby, but she had a sneaking suspicion that coffee with Leo was off. This had the potential to be a huge break in the case.

Laurence was ushered back into the depths of the station, and sure enough, a few minutes later, Leo texted Vicki again.

So, so, so sorry, he said. *Just got the information that I need for a search warrant. Can we take a rain check?*

She typed, *Of course. No worries.*

But she did have worries. Many worries.

She drove home, her thoughts churning on the case. When she got back, she kept her eyes open for anything suspicious, but everything seemed fine as she let herself inside. No attackers were lurking in her bushes. She fed Sunny and then went into the kitchen and stared at the ingredients for her scrubs.

She should make another batch. She started grinding the herbs but kept stopping to check her phone. What was happening with the case? Where was Leo searching? The festival warehouse? Julia's house?

Oh, and she still had to go to the reading of the will as James's legal representative tomorrow. She groaned out loud. After twenty minutes of halfheartedly mixing a scrub, she gave up and flopped on the couch. Her headache was definitely getting worse from all this stress.

Not too long after, Leo called.

"Hey," she answered on the first ring, her pulse pounding in her throat.

"Hey," he said, his voice soft and sad. "I've got some news on the case for you."

"Oh? Didn't think you were giving me updates," she replied.

"Well, this isn't so much an update as closure."

Her faint hope winked out of existence like a snuffed candle. They'd found something when they'd executed the search warrant, then. "Tell me," she said, nausea welling up in her stomach.

He took a deep breath. "I'm sorry it ended this way, Vick, but we were alerted to a life insurance policy benefiting James and Julia and their mom. We got a warrant to search Julia's house and found arsenic —like what was used to poison Kristen."

Vicki frowned. "Where was the arsenic?"

"Hidden in a vase on the entryway table."

"Okay. Thanks for calling."

"Just so you know, we've arrested Julia. The DA is drawing up charges. It's over, Vick. I really am sorry."

"Glad you figured it out! I'm just making a scrub. Talk to you later." She hung up as fast as she could so that she wouldn't burst into tears on the phone.

CHAPTER 16

Though Vicki only slept in fits and spurts that night, she attacked scrub-making the next morning with a vengeance. She made a cranberry scrub and an energizing scrub and a relaxing scrub.

But not even the lavender oil in the relaxing scrub helped her feel relaxed. Not even a little bit.

"How could I have been so stupid?" she groaned to herself as she stirred the newest batch. "I started falling for a murderer *again*, but this time I should have known better. I *knew* he was a murder suspect."

Maybe she was meant to be single for the rest of her life. She apparently had terrible taste in men. Or maybe she really *should* just start writing love letters to imprisoned serial killers—with her track record, any guy she fell for was probably a murderer anyway.

She put more astragalus in the mortar and crushed it into submission with the pestle.

The whole story made so much sense. James and Julia, concerned for their mom's long-term care and knowing that Frank didn't really have the money to get the treatments she needed, hatched a plot to kill him for the life insurance money. Then, when the police immediately arrested James, Julia offed Kristen to make it look like the killer was still on the loose.

"Why am I even making scrubs?" Vicki muttered. "It's not like the Fall Festival is still going to happen with the chair dead and the deputy chair arrested."

But she needed somewhere to vent her anxious energy.

She attacked the astragalus with the pestle again. "Maybe I should just go back to being a lawyer," she half-yelled. "Steady job, steady paycheck, and best of all, very little free time to think about men."

She stopped grinding the astragalus and stared at it. Maybe she really should go back to being a lawyer. Her gaze flicked to the window, to the beehives beyond. Did she *want* to do this anymore? The thought of ramping up her struggling business, of trying to make this work . . . that sounded more exhausting than the long, soul-sucking hours of lawyering.

Especially because this business was now so tied up in her romantic failures with Alexander and James. When she looked at the half-finished scrub, all she could see were memories of her terrible judgment calls.

Plus, the Fall Festival was definitely going to be canceled, so it wasn't like she was getting the influx of cash she'd expected. Maybe Claire, that bee-venom woman, knew a good beekeeper who could give her bees a great new home.

With a groan, Vicki abandoned the half-ground astragalus and stalked up the stairs to her bedroom. Without changing into pajamas, she collapsed into bed and pulled the comforter over her head to hide from the world.

Then the phone rang. It was Mona.

"Hey," said Mona, her voice gentle. "I heard about the arrest. Are you coming to Coupon Clippers?"

"No," Vicki groaned, nestling deeper into the blankets. "I'm exploring a new career as a professional burrito."

"Well, you need to come," said Mona, getting a little more forceful. "You need to focus on something else for a little bit. Remember what Aunt Bee said? Clipping coupons is the best therapy."

Well, I won't need to clip coupons much longer. I won't need to pinch every penny if I'm going back to being a lawyer. There's a job with a steady paycheck, even if it does drain my soul.

And she *was* going back to being a lawyer, she realized. Because she just couldn't do this honey business anymore, and she didn't have enough savings to start up something brand-new.

The realization opened up a hole in her chest, but there was a sense of relief about it too. Closure. She hadn't been able to get her business off the ground, but there was no shame in that. Most small businesses failed.

But she'd go to Coupon Clippers today to satisfy Mona and Aunt Bee, so they wouldn't worry so much about her. Plus, the reading of the will was later that afternoon, so she needed to do *something* to pull herself together.

"Fiiiiiiine," she groaned. "What time is it again?"

"Meeting starts at eleven fifteen, which is an hour from now."

"See you there." Vicki hung up. She stayed in her blanket burrito for another minute, and then reluctantly headed into the bathroom and turned on the shower.

An hour later, she walked into the Coupon Clippers meeting with a brave smile and enough concealer to hide the bags under her eyes.

"Vicki!" Aunt Bee bustled across the meeting room to give her a hug, Mona right behind her. "Are you all right?"

With an Oscar-worthy effort at acting, Vicki kept the smile on her face. "You know, it was a disappointment—I really misjudged the case. But it's not like Julia and I were ever the best of friends, so I'm not heartbroken or anything."

Mona quirked an eyebrow, but Vicki mouthed, "Let it be," and shook her head slightly.

Aunt Bee released Vicki from the maternal embrace, saying, "Well, I'm glad to hear that. You'd just put so much effort into solving the case."

Vicki found a seat across from Sheldon and Alana, who were holding hands and sneaking glances at each other. Her heart stuttered at the sight of the happy couple. She was so very glad for them, but it was another reminder of the failures of her love life . . . of how she'd harbored a desperate, hidden hope that, after the case was solved, she might walk down the street holding hands with James.

She swallowed past her turmoil and fixed a fake grin on Alana. "How are you doing?"

"Great!" said Alana. "Really shocking about Julia being arrested, though, wasn't it?"

Sheldon nodded grimly.

Vicki managed a little shrug as Mona sat next to her. "Not what I expected, but it sounds like the evidence is pretty convincing."

With a little shake of his head, Sheldon said, "Really too bad. I do hope their mother is all right after all of this. What a tragedy—your husband murdered by your two children. And she's ill by all accounts too."

"Bedridden," Vicki said. "With chronic Lyme. She does have a sister, at least, who I think will do her best to take care of her."

But Sheldon was right. The whole thing was absolutely tragic. Would James and Julia's mom be able to handle it in her current state of health?

Vicki chided herself. Here she'd been so focused on feeling sorry for herself, when Rose's whole life had been ruined by everything that had happened. She turned to Mona. "Oh, I told Claire I want to donate the first month of bee venom, so that people who really need the treatment and can't afford it can get it discounted."

"Oh?" said Mona, her face showing her concern. "Even with the festival probably canceled? You need that money."

Less than you'd think, now. But Vicki just shrugged. "Well, I promised the pro bono venom before Julia was arrested, and I can't very well back out now. I was thinking about Rose when I offered it, actually. Part of the deal I struck with Claire was that Rose would be on the list for discounted treatment, if she wants it."

Alana glanced from Vicki to Mona. "Bee venom?"

"Yeah," said Vicki. "There's a doctor in Pigeon Hollow who uses bee venom to treat some long-term conditions. Chronic Lyme is one of her specialties, I guess. Says she sees patients 'literally get their lives back.' Anyway, she caught me at Mona's store and asked if I'd sell her some venom. She has a way of collecting it so that it doesn't kill any bees."

"Fascinating!" Alana said. "Speaking of bees, in happier news, your blog feature is scheduled to go live very early tomorrow morning!"

The blog feature! Vicki had almost forgotten.

Alana continued, "My posts always go live at three thirty a.m., because *Frugalicious* readers are often early risers, and I always want it ready before they wake up. You know, that bee-venom thing sounds really interesting. I'm going to do a little research first, but if I like what I see, do you mind if I add that angle to the post? Talk about what you're doing with donating the first month of venom?"

"Whatever you think is best," said Vicki absentmindedly. Her thoughts churned. Should she really close down the business? She might not have the Fall Festival to sell her products, but she might make some money off that blog feature . . .

But, no. She was serious about closing down. Should she ask Alana to cancel the blog post? She wavered for half a second before she had a better idea.

"You know," she said brightly, "I've actually changed my mind about the sale price for the scrubs—I have too many of them, now that we won't be able to sell them at the festival. If it's not too much trouble, could you edit the post to say that all of my products are fifty percent off, while supplies last?"

Mona eyed Vicki suspiciously.

"Oh, definitely!" said Alana. "My readers will love that."

Mona held out a hand. "Vicki . . ."

But Vicki ignored her and pulled up her online store on her phone to set all the products to a half-off sale. *It's a good way to close out the store. A clearance sale. That way, I hopefully won't be left with a huge inventory that I'll have to throw away. And maybe I can even use some of the profits to help out Rose and Kelly. I won't need them if I'm taking a job as an attorney soon.*

"Do thirty-five percent," said Mona firmly. "You need to make money on the scrubs. You've put a lot of time into them."

Vicki glanced at Alana, who shrugged.

"How about a buy-one-get-one for the lip balms and thirty-five percent off everything else?" offered Alana.

"Sounds good," said Vicki, entering the correct information into the sales app. Then she turned off notifications—no need for her phone to ding every time someone ordered a discount lip balm. She'd check the orders in batches for a day or two after the blog post went live.

Would her old law firm take her back, or would she have to apply around to others? There were only two firms in Magnolia Falls. If she couldn't find a job here, she'd have to look in neighboring towns. Would she have to move away from her family and friends? The thought sent another wave of panic clawing through her chest.

"Ah-hem." Aunt Bee cleared her throat loudly. "I'd like to call this meeting to order."

Sheldon dropped Alana's hand so he could begin taking notes, and then they glanced at each other and switched seats so that Sheldon could take notes with his right hand and hold Alana's with his left.

"Our last meeting was here in the library just a few days ago," continued Aunt Bee. "Attending members were myself, Mona, Vicki, Sheldon, Alana, Tia, Pepe, and . . . Julia."

Everyone let out a sad little sigh at the mention of Julia.

Vicki's thoughts drifted as Aunt Bee warbled on, addressing past and current business. Once Aunt Bee stopped talking, Mona nudged Vicki.

"Coupons?" Mona asked, holding out a stack of magazine pages.

"Thanks," said Vicki, her throat tight.

She clipped a few coupons, but the emotion kept building in her chest. She needed to get out of here—needed a chance to gather herself, away from these warm, happy faces. She *had* to keep up a professional face during the reading of the will.

Abruptly, she stood. "I have to head out now," she said. "Thank you so much for the coupons. But I'm actually doing a little legal work for a friend, and I have to prep before a meeting."

Mona followed Vicki out, but as soon as they left the meeting room, Vicki waved her back.

"I have to represent James at the reading of the will, because I agreed to do it," she whispered, her voice trembling. "I have to collect myself, and I need to do that alone."

Mona rested a comforting hand on Vicki's shoulder. "Call me after? I'm worried about you."

Vicki nodded.

Then Mona turned and headed back to the Coupon Clippers.

Vicki practically ran out of the library, only relaxing when she closed and locked her car door. She leaned her head back against the seat. She had an hour and thirty minutes before the reading of the will.

First, she stopped off at Tiger Forest Coffee Shop and ordered a cappuccino. She sat in the window, watching the sunlight as it danced on the autumn leaves and sipping the delicious cinnamon-and-coffee foam. She glanced at her phone screen. An hour left.

I'll go to the courthouse early, she decided.

When she'd argued cases in court in the past, she'd always liked to get there early to get the feel of the building—and sometimes of the courtroom itself if she had the good luck to be the first case of the day. It had always grounded her, helped her feel prepared for what she was about to do.

She walked into the county courthouse and took a slow, deep breath, savoring the familiar place. The paintings on the walls. The smell of stale cigarettes that didn't seem to go away even though the building had been non-smoking for years. The statue of Lady Justice with her sword and scales.

When she reached the officer standing guard, she said, "Excuse me —I'm one of the family member's attorneys—could you tell me where the will is being read?"

He eyed her suspiciously, no doubt recognizing her as Leo's little sister, but pointed to a room down the hall.

Before she went that way, Vicki decided to head to the restroom to freshen up. She ran a comb through her hair and fixed the mascara that had smudged under her eyes. She was just about to leave when she heard all-too-familiar voices right outside the door. *Laurence and Linda!*

The bathroom door started to open, and Vicki bolted into a stall, closing and locking the door just as Linda walked in. Her heart hammered. She'd see them at the reading of the will, of course, but she really didn't want to deal with a confrontation and explanation in the bathroom before anything got started.

Wait, is Linda humming? Vicki tilted her head and watched Linda through the crack in the stall door.

The woman strode to the counter with a skip in her step, then took off her jacket and set it next to the sink. She seemed to be reaching for something in her purse.

Something was different about Linda. *She seems awfully upbeat . . .*

Every other time, she'd seemed absolutely devastated by her dad's death, like she was always a breath away from bawling her eyes out.

Then a smell hit Vicki's nostrils, and she blinked. Calamine lotion? Any beekeeper worth her salt would know that smell all too well. She shifted to try to get a better view of Linda.

And she froze when she saw Linda putting calamine lotion on several welts on her left arm.

Welts that looked suspiciously like bee stings.

CHAPTER 17

a s soon as Linda left the restroom, Vicki let out a long breath. Linda had bee stings on her arm—which meant she'd attacked Vicki. There would be no reason to attack Vicki unless . . .

Unless she'd been involved in the murders and became afraid I was closing in.

"But the life insurance policy and the arsenic in Julia's house," she whispered. Then the realization hit her. Laurence and Linda had seemed startled when Vicki had followed them into the entryway to grab her jacket. They were right by the entryway table. Had they been planting the poison? Had they been afraid she'd seen them put something in the vase? Is that why they'd followed Vicki home and attacked her?

Plus, did James and Julia even need that money to take care of their mom? James *had* said he'd offered to help out with the treatments and had been turned down. And Julia had offered to pay for a live-in nurse. Frank might have been close to broke, but James and Julia weren't.

Vicki cautiously crept to the bathroom door and opened it, peering up and down the hallway. No sign of Laurence or Linda. She dialed Aunt Bee.

"Yes, dear?" Aunt Bee said. "Do you need something? I'm just walking into the grocery store—I found a great coupon for ready-made tuna salad. Did you know that just one serving of fish—"

"Aunt Bee, sorry to interrupt, but I need a favor," said Vicki, grimacing.

"Anything, dear," warbled Aunt Bee.

You haven't heard what I'm going to ask yet.

"I need you to go down to the jail and bail out Julia." Her voice cracked on the last word.

"I'm sorry, say that again, dear?"

"I'm serious," said Vicki. "I really need you to bail out Julia. Things aren't what they seem. I just found something big. Something that's going to prove I was right, and that James and Julia aren't guilty."

Aunt Bee gasped. "Did you really? That's wonderful. I'll go there right away."

Vicki let out a little sigh of relief. "Thank you for trusting me."

Aunt Bee certainly had the money to bail out Julia, but she was very careful with every dollar she had. That she would go post bail without second-guessing Vicki . . . well, that meant a lot.

Next, Vicki called Leo.

"Hey, Vick, what's up?"

"Leo," she said. "I need you to listen very carefully to me and not interrupt."

His voice sounded more alert. "Sure. What's up? Are you safe?"

"Yes, I'm safe," she said. "But I just figured something out about the case."

He sighed. "Vick, I'm really sorry things didn't turn out the way you wanted, but—"

"Leo, listen!" she hissed. "The person who attacked me is still on the loose, and they're in the same building as me."

That got his attention. "Wait, what? Tell me everything."

"Look into Laurence and Linda Young," she said.

"Frank's kids?"

"Yes. Find out what day they really arrived here from Colorado, and if either of them rented a silver sedan at any point. And when Aunt Bee comes to bail out Julia, no stalling. Let her out as fast as you possibly can, and tell her to go straight to the reading of the will at the courthouse. I'm going to stall them as long as I can, but it's starting soon."

She hung up before he could ask her more questions, then took a deep breath and looked at her reflection in the mirror. "You can do this," she said. "Just another case."

But it wasn't. She'd gotten emotionally invested. Everything was riding on this.

She hoped she was right.

She waited a couple more minutes, then left the restroom and strode to the designated meeting room. She peered through the window set in the door. Kelly, Laurence, Linda, and a man she didn't recognize were all waiting inside.

Laurence and Linda had smug smiles on their faces. Kelly's hands were folded, her knuckles white.

A black-suited man walked past Vicki into the room, shooting her a questioning look. The lawyer who was doing the reading, no doubt.

"Can we get started?" asked Linda, studying her white-tipped nails.

The lawyer glanced at the door, and Vicki walked in.

"Not quite yet," declared Vicki. "We're waiting for one more person, and it's not yet time for the reading of the will to start."

Linda sneered in Vicki's direction. "What are *you* doing here?"

"And who are we waiting for?" retorted Laurence.

"I'm here representing James," said Vicki, shooting an apologetic glance at Kelly. But Kelly just seemed relieved that she didn't have to do this alone.

"Don't you have to be a lawyer to do that?" demanded Laurence, crossing his arms.

"I *am* a lawyer," Vicki retorted.

Laurence and Linda looked uncomfortable but composed themselves and conferred quietly with the other man—their own lawyer, Vicki presumed.

Vicki sat at the desk and stared at the clock as the minutes ticked by. She willed Julia to hurry.

When the clock reached 1:02, the presiding lawyer glanced at Vicki and said, "We really do need to get started."

"Absolutely," said Vicki. "Permission to briefly confer with my client's family?"

"It's time to get started!" exclaimed the lawyer for Laurence and Linda.

Vicki mouthed, "Please."

The presiding lawyer shrugged. "Sure. Don't take too long."

Vicki grabbed Kelly's hand and pulled her out of the room.

"What's happening?" Kelly asked quietly.

Vicki closed the door and whispered, "Julia's on her way."

"Julia?" Kelly's eyes brightened. "She made bail?"

"We're getting it posted for her right now," said Vicki. "I'm stalling until she's able to get here. She needs to be here for the reading. As soon as that lawyer comes out here and tells us to get started, tell him you have a bathroom emergency and stay in the bathroom for five minutes."

Kelly nodded solemnly.

Two minutes ticked by. Vicki's phone buzzed with a text from Leo: *Julia's on her way. I hope you know what you're doing.*

Vicki showed the text to Kelly. "She'll be here in five minutes," she whispered.

The presiding attorney poked his head out of the room. "Are you about ready?" he asked, impatience thickening his voice.

"Just a minute!" cried Kelly. "Ladies' room emergency, if you catch my drift!" Kelly practically ran in the direction of the restroom. Vicki could have given her a standing ovation.

The presiding attorney fixed a dubious stare on Vicki. "What on earth are you doing?" he demanded.

"Kelly just needed to use the restroom," said Vicki innocently. "Unrelated, Julia Hewitt will be here in less than five minutes. I'll be very happy to begin the second she's here."

He let out an exasperated sigh. "Five minutes, and then we're starting regardless of who is or isn't in the room. Got it?"

"Got it," she said as he retreated.

She followed him in and took a seat across the table from Laurence and Linda.

"Who are you?" demanded Laurence. "Why do you keep showing up?"

But Vicki didn't reply. She didn't owe him an explanation.

Four minutes later, Julia and Kelly bustled into the room. Julia's hair was uncombed, and her face showed her exhaustion, but she looked . . . like she had hope. The women took the two seats on either side of Vicki.

"Now we can get started," said Vicki. "We're all here."

"Well, if we are *finally* ready to begin, I'll read the last will and testament," said the presiding attorney as he sat behind the main desk.

His voice droned as he read through all the legalese, but it wasn't hard to interpret. The will had been last updated eleven months earlier. Everything was left to Laurence and Linda, except the paintings, which were to go to his wife and James and Julia, with the money to go first and foremost to pay for Rose's medical bills, with James and Julia as joint beneficiaries so that they could access it easily if their mom became fully incapacitated.

"Those hideous things? They won't fetch anything in the market," Julia hissed. Vicki put her hand on Julia's arm to quiet her.

Laurence and Linda were furiously whispering with their lawyer.

"He left instructions to take them to a specific dealer for appraisal," said the presiding attorney, handing Julia a card with the dealer's name and address. "He made the arrangements a while ago, and the will is quite clear that you are not to use anyone else."

"How dare he!" yelled Laurence. All heads turned in his direction.

"I cannot believe he left those paintings to *her*," said Linda.

Vicki raised a brow. By all accounts, the paintings weren't worth much. Was this about their sentimental value?

Laurence stood up and turned to Julia. "We'll fight you in court."

"Why?" asked Julia. "As far as I'm concerned, you can have them."

Vicki blurted, "No, they cannot. The paintings are now jointly the property of Julia, Rose, and my client. Frank's instructions were clear, and my client won't make any decisions until they've been appraised." Then she turned to Julia and added in a low murmur, "Hold onto them for now, until we've figured out what's going on."

"I guess," said Julia skeptically.

But Vicki knew something was up. Why would Linda have attacked her? These two were definitely shady.

"You cannot sell them," insisted Linda tearfully, but the sentiment sounded fake and forced. "Tell them they cannot sell *my* dad's paintings."

The siblings' lawyer rubbed his temples and looked like he wanted to be anywhere else.

"Do you intend to contest the will?" asked the presiding attorney.

"Yes," said Laurence and Linda in unison.

CHAPTER 18

"*I* think that's the last of it," Vicki said as she and Julia finished carrying Frank's treasure trove of art into the dealer's gallery the next morning.

"Mr. Lopez will be with you in just a moment," said a young assistant before disappearing toward the back of the gallery.

Julia glanced at Vicki. "Still not sure what the point of all this is."

"Well," replied Vicki, "you can't sell them while the will is being contested, of course, but nothing wrong with getting them appraised —and this is the dealer Frank specified in the will."

Julia shrugged and muttered, "I don't even know what Frank was thinking toward the end of his life. I didn't even know he had a life insurance policy."

"Yup," said Vicki.

Julia scowled at a nearby statue. "I mean, it's nice that he was thinking of us and all, but if he thought these paintings would fetch enough money to pay for Mom's continued care . . . he was losing it."

But Vicki's mind was still circling on Julia's previous statement: *I didn't even know he had a life insurance policy.*

Vicki had seen the policy when Laurence had waved it at her— conveniently, the agent was an old family friend. *Small towns for the win.*

As she'd looked through Frank's documentation on behalf of James the night before, she'd been startled to realize that Frank only had about ten thousand dollars in assets that were all his own, besides the paintings. Everything else was a joint asset with Rose, which she got to keep. Laurence and Linda were inheriting about five thousand apiece. But the will had been amended recently—less than a year ago. Eleven months, to be exact. And the insurance policy had been amended even more recently—eight months ago. Was that all a coincidence?

On a hunch, she stepped outside and called the insurance agent. "Hey, Tom, how are you?" she asked when he answered.

"Oh, pretty good," said Tom. He was a middle-aged man whose daughter had been in the same class as Vicki and Mona. "How are you doing? I heard about the fire at Mona's store."

They chatted for about a minute, and then she said, "So, I'm actually calling with a professional question. I'm representing a client who I really believe has been wrongly charged with murder."

"Oh!" exclaimed Tom. "Well, you don't hear that every day, do you?"

"The deceased actually bought a life insurance policy through you," Vicki continued.

"Oh, this is on the Frank Young murder?" asked Tom.

"Yes," said Vicki, pacing up and down the sidewalk. "I noticed that the policy beneficiaries were changed fairly recently. Did Frank ever mention anything to you about why he was doing that?"

"Oh, his children talked him into it," said Tom.

Vicki stopped cold. "Do you mean his stepchildren?"

"No, his own kids. Larry and . . . Leah, or something?"

"Laurence and Linda."

"Yes," he exclaimed. "Those are the names. Live in Colorado, I think. Anyway, they were the previous beneficiaries. They were home for a visit, and it sounded like they'd persuaded him that, if anything happened to him, the money should go to his sick wife. Two or three times at the signing, he asked them if they were sure he was doing the right thing, but they absolutely insisted. Nice people."

Not so nice as it seems. Vicki's mind turned on this new information.

Why would Laurence and Linda have acted like the life insurance beneficiary information was a surprise to them? She walked back toward the gallery.

"Thanks so much, Tom," she said. "This has been very helpful."

She hung up as she pushed open the door to the gallery. Julia was standing next to a thirtysomething man who was wearing spectacles and a suit that was slightly too short through the arms. He was pointing to something in the corner of the painting, and Julia let out a shriek.

Heart pounding, Vicki ran to them. "What's wrong?"

Julia could only stutter in response.

The dealer let out a chuckle. "I had some very good news for her. Frank was a little bit of a peculiar guy. He enjoyed painting, but he was under no illusions about his own talent. He picked it up as a way of hiding an inheritance he'd gotten from his uncle."

His uncle! "Jack," Vicki said. "Jack, who always had . . . the best stories."

James's words flashed through her head: *If you believed him, he once danced with Princess Diana in Australia. But I doubt it. He also said that a wolf once led him to a cache of diamonds buried near his cabin in Alaska and that the agent James Bond was based on rescued him from pirates off the coast of Africa. You'd believe anything while he was talking to you, though.*

"Diamonds!" cried Julia. "He hid diamonds in the paintings!"

Diamonds? Vicki's stomach flipped.

The dealer gestured to one of the paintings—a landscape under a starry night. "See, here in the top-right corner, beneath the stars— that's not just thick paint." He nicked a little chunk of paint off with his thumbnail, revealing a gleaming, cut diamond beneath.

Vicki let out an audible gasp.

The dealer continued, "About a dozen of the paintings have the diamonds. All told, the diamonds are worth about three million dollars. Those paintings were the ones he priced so high—high enough that he knew he wouldn't get buyers for them. As he practiced, he got better, and I encouraged him to try to sell some of his very newest paintings. The ones without diamonds, of course. He was going to set those at reasonable prices. I offered to show one of them here in the gallery."

"But . . . but . . ." Julia stuttered. "Why? Why go to the trouble of hiding diamonds in a painting? Why not . . . put them in a safety-deposit box like a normal person? Or sell them?"

"He lost his money in a bad stock purchase," said Vicki slowly. "That's what Laurence and Linda said."

"So?" asked Julia.

"So, he didn't trust banks," murmured Vicki. "And I don't think he trusted his kids either. For good reason, as it turns out."

The dealer nodded. "He didn't spell everything out for me, but he did express concern about keeping it absolutely secret until after his death, when I would be free to tell his wife or his stepkids, but not his own kids."

"And he inherited all this from Uncle Jack?" Julia asked in wonder.

"I believe so. He told me that he'd kept them in a sock underneath his mattress for a few years, but wanted to put them somewhere safer."

Julia snorted.

"I wasn't sure that hiding them in paintings was especially safe, but he—"

"Wait," interjected Vicki. "When did you first see the diamonds? When did he come to you?"

The dealer quirked his lips in thought. "Well, almost a year ago, I think? Oh! It was right before Christmas, so just about ten months."

Ten months. Vicki pressed her hands together. A month after the will was last updated, and two months before Laurence and Linda talked their father into changing the beneficiaries of the life insurance policy.

"Do you have a safe you can put these in?" Vicki asked. "Frank's kids know about the diamonds. I'm sure of it. That's why they want the paintings so badly."

He nodded somberly. "Of course. I'll put them in it for safekeeping."

The final pieces clicked together in Vicki's head. She turned to Julia. "I've figured it out. We're going to the police station."

CHAPTER 19

"*V*ick, could you please explain what's going on?" Leo asked in exasperation.

"Not a chance." She grinned at him. "I'm savoring this."

They were standing in the lobby of the police station with Julia and Leo's partner, Detective Kimura.

A moment later, the door opened and Mona walked in. "Are you okay?" she asked Vicki.

Vicki smiled. "I just wanted you here for this."

Mona shared a questioning look with Leo, but he just shrugged at her.

After a few minutes, the door opened again, and Laurence and Linda strolled in, dressed in all black. They stopped, eyes darting from Leo to Vicki to Julia.

"What is this about?" demanded Laurence.

"I've got a story that you might find interesting," said Vicki. "A story about what really happened to your dad."

They crossed their arms and glared at her.

She continued, "Frank lost his money in the stock market and didn't have too much trust in banks as a result. So, when he inherited a cache of diamonds worth millions from your great-uncle—

diamonds Uncle Jack had found on his property up north—he didn't sell them or put them in a safety-deposit box. Instead, he hid them."

A look of rage flickered across Linda's face, but she seemed to catch herself. "Dad had diamonds?" she asked, feigning surprise.

Vicki ignored her. "As Rose got sicker, he became increasingly concerned about her long-term care. He also became concerned that, if he died, his children would do whatever they could to cut Rose out of the money. Because the diamonds were an inheritance, they were legally his own property, not community property with Rose. So he hatched a plan to hide the diamonds where the two of you"—she pointed at Laurence and Linda—"wouldn't find them, and to structure his will in such a way that you thought you were inheriting everything he had."

They didn't say anything.

Vicki glanced at Leo. "But Frank didn't know that they'd found out about the diamonds. Somehow, they figured out that Jack's stories— or that one, at least—were actually true, and that Jack had willed all those diamonds to their father. They came out to visit, and Frank mentioned that he'd recently changed his will—that he was leaving the paintings to Rose, Julia, and James, but that Laurence and Linda would get all his assets. And somehow, on that visit, Laurence and Linda figured out that Frank was hiding his diamonds in the artwork."

"This is a crazy story," cried Laurence. "You can't possibly believe a word of this, Detective. She has no proof."

Looking straight at Laurence and Linda, Vicki continued, "When you realized that you were being cut out in favor of Frank's second wife and stepkids, you hatched a plan. You didn't intend to kill him— not at first. You really did love him, didn't you?"

Tears glimmered in Linda's eyes.

"You began to profess how very concerned you were for Rose. You knew there was a small life insurance policy—fifty-thousand dollars— and that you were the beneficiaries. You also knew the diamonds were worth far, far more than the value of the policy. So you decided to try to manipulate your father into giving you the inheritance you believed was rightfully yours. If you could convince him that you cared about Rose—if he thought he'd misjudged you, that you weren't greedy, that you'd make sure his wife was taken care of, he might give the diamonds to you. Or at least some of them. You persuaded him to change the insurance policy, but he didn't change the will. You were still cut out of any real inheritance."

Laurence's face reddened, and his jaw ticked with barely restrained rage.

"Well, this is interesting," murmured Leo.

"But I'm not done," said Vicki, still staring at Laurence and Linda. "Like I said, the two of you loved your father. But sometimes love runs awfully close to hate, doesn't it? You felt betrayed. You'd been so devoted to him, and now he was favoring his second family—favoring his wife's children over his own children. And maybe you did have a right to be angry." Her voice was softer now. "Maybe it wasn't fair that he left all of it to Rose and none of it to you."

Now a tear tracked down Linda's cheek.

"But you didn't have the right to kill him," said Vicki.

Linda opened her mouth to retort, but Laurence clapped a hand on her arm.

Vicki continued, "Fueled by rage, you made a final, devastating plan—a plan to reclaim your inheritance and to get revenge on the man who'd betrayed you. You started by killing him in the park where you knew James went running every afternoon. Then you killed Kristen to throw blame on Julia, too. After all, Julia was the only common thread between Kristen and Frank. Once they were convicted of the murder plot, they wouldn't be able to inherit anything—which left only Rose. It'd have been so easy to sneak in and smother her in her sleep, wouldn't it?"

Julia's jaw dropped, and molten rage smoldered in her eyes as she stared at her stepsiblings.

"She's been so sick," said Vicki, "and it's such an easy story—the trauma of her husband's death and her two children arrested for murder just did her in. It wouldn't have looked like another murder. People would have thought that she'd died of natural causes. And you almost added another murder when you attacked me. You worried I'd witnessed you planting the arsenic at Julia's house, so you followed me home and whacked me over the head when I was harvesting bees.

Unfortunately, Linda still has the stings on her left arm, which is going to look pretty bad to a jury."

"There's no proof," muttered Laurence.

Leo stepped forward. "I did find it interesting that plane ticket records show you actually arrived in the state the day before Frank's death, however. You told us that you came in after you got the news. Why'd you lie? And why did you rent a silver sedan two days ago—right before Vicki was attacked by someone driving a silver sedan—and return it within a couple hours?"

The siblings both stood there, practically shaking.

"Give it up," said Vicki softly. "The jury will go easier on you if you confess."

"You're wrong!" yelled Linda. Laurence nudged her, but tears streamed down her face, and she kept going. "Kristen wasn't supposed to die, and we weren't going to kill Rose! Julia was supposed to die."

"Quiet!" hissed Laurence.

But Linda just shook her head. "I'm sorry," she said. "We were going to plant a suicide note that said Julia regretted her part in the murder plot, that James had killed Frank and that Rose was in on it. We figured Rose wouldn't be charged, because she's so sick they wouldn't be able to prove she fully understood it. But she wouldn't be able to inherit the paintings."

Leo let out a long whistle, and he and his partner moved toward Laurence and Linda.

"Well," said Leo as he clapped handcuffs on Laurence. "You're under arrest for the murders of Frank Young and Kristen Smith. You have the right to remain silent. Anything you say can and will be used against you in a court of law. You have the right to an attorney . . ."

As Leo continued reading their rights, Julia turned to Vicki, amazement on her face.

"You . . . you did it," she said. "James is cleared!" Then she bowled into Vicki and gave her a huge hug. "I can't thank you enough."

Mona threw her arms around them, completing the group hug.

When Julia pulled back, tears shone in her eyes. "Well, I guess you can definitely sell your honey and jam in the Fall Festival," she quipped.

CHAPTER 20

icki, Mona, and Julia piled in Vicki's car. "Next stop, jail!" sang Vicki. "We're breaking James out!"

Leo had promised them that by the time they got there, the jail staff would know that James was to be released immediately.

"Hey." From the back seat, Mona poked Julia's arm. "James is single, right?"

"Yup," said Julia. "Broke up with his last girlfriend four or five months ago. And I was glad. She was the worst."

Vicki chuckled. "Do you think everyone is the worst?"

Julia paused, a grimace on her face. "I do come across that way, don't I? I should really be better about that. But yes, this particular girlfriend *was* the worst."

"Well," drawled Mona. "Conveniently, Vicki's last boyfriend was also the worst, so maybe they can bond over that."

"Are you interested in James?" Julia asked Vicki, her brow furrowed.

Vicki scowled at Mona in the rearview mirror. "We knew each other a little in high school," she replied noncommittally. "I thought he was cute then, and I've enjoyed talking to him as I've poked around on the case."

Julia seemed to consider this. "You should ask him out."

Vicki paused with her hand on the gear shift and looked at Julia quizzically. "Wait, are you serious?"

"Yeah," Julia said with a small smile. "I think I am. You're . . . you're a good person, Vicki. I'm *not* a nice person, and I know that. I do want to try to be better. But even after I kept you out of the festival last year and was unkind to you recently, you still worked to prove my brother's innocence—and mine. Thank you."

Vicki shared a wide-eyed look with Mona.

"See!" cried Mona. "You've got to ask him out."

An idea formed in Vicki's head. She gave Mona a sly grin. "Tell you what. I'll ask out James if you ask out Leo."

A furious blush bloomed on Mona's cheeks. "Oh, I couldn't do that," she protested.

"Why not?" asked Vicki. "We'll make it a double date. I insist. Leo's going to meet us at the jail to officially apologize to James."

Mona grimaced, her cheeks still flaming red. "Well . . . all right, I guess."

Vicki threw the car into gear and pulled out of the parking lot. *No doubt Mona will chicken out at the last moment, so I might just have to ask him for her.* "By the way, Julia," she said, "have you ever heard of bee-venom therapy?"

Julia's forehead wrinkled. "No, I can't say I have."

Vicki said, "Well, I've got another surprise for you . . ."

She told the story, and Julia said, "Oh, I'm sure Mom will want to try it! She'll try anything at this point. But you don't have to donate the venom on our behalf—the diamonds will more than pay for whatever treatments she needs. Save the donated venom for someone who's in financial straits."

They arrived at the jail, and Julia ran inside ahead of them. When Vicki and Mona walked through the doors, James was already in the lobby, and Julia had embraced him in a tight hug.

Julia's voice was thick with emotion as she said, "It was Laurence and Linda. They killed Frank and Kristen and tried to pin it on us. I thought I wasn't going to see you again. Thought we were both going to jail for the rest of our lives. But everything's all right now." Then she stepped back, wiped away her tears, and gestured with her head.

"Thanks to Vicki. She believed in us and didn't stop until she figured out the truth."

James gave Vicki a smile that made her weak at the knees. "I don't know how to thank you," he said.

Vicki opened her mouth to reply, but the door opened behind her, and Leo walked in. He strode up to James and shook his hand.

"You're officially cleared in the investigation of Frank's death, and I'd like to offer the department's sincere apology. The killers tried to set you up, and we fell for it. I'm sorry." Then Leo turned to Vicki. "I owe you an apology, too, Vick. You saw the truth when I couldn't, and I tried to keep you from working on the case. But your instincts were right all along."

Your instincts were right all along. James wasn't another Alexander. An unexpected lump of emotion swelled in her throat. She could leave that ghost in the past now.

"Three cheers for Vicki!" cried Julia.

Everyone clapped and whooped, and Vicki just shook her head with a huge smile on her face.

When the cheers died down, Vicki looked at James with a little smile. "I was wondering if you might want to do something tomorrow afternoon? We could maybe grab coffee and walk by the river?"

His smile was absolutely dazzling. "That sounds amazing."

Vicki nudged Mona and cleared her throat, but Mona just stared at the floor. So Vicki added, "Leo, why don't you and Mona come along too? That could be fun."

Leo's eyes widened, and a faint blush reddened his ears. "Uh, yeah. Sure. Yeah," he stuttered. "That'd be great."

Vicki's phone buzzed, and she checked it to find a text from Alana. *The blog post is getting tons of views and clicks,* it said. *How are your sales?*

Her heart jumped into her throat as she opened her sales app, then let out a little shriek.

"What is it?" demanded Mona.

Vicki read and reread the numbers on her screen. That couldn't be right. Her pulse pounded. Was she misunderstanding? Was there a glitch in the system? She took a deep breath and turned the phone to show Mona.

Mona covered her mouth and half-screamed. "Oh my gosh! Is that from the blog post?"

Vicki nodded slowly. "I . . . think it is."

"What?" Leo asked, looking half-alarmed.

"Vicki's sold thousands of dollars of products today!" exclaimed Mona. "Alana featured her on *Frugalicious*!"

"Thousands of dollars," said Vicki, raking a hand through her hair, "and everything was discounted! That's way more product than I have in stock! And the Fall Festival is coming up in a week! How will I possibly . . ." She turned to James, eyes wide. "I'm so sorry. I'm going to need to take a rain check on hanging out. I'm going to be working nonstop on making scrubs and lip balm and harvesting honey!"

"Do you need help?" asked James. "How about we just change the location. We can hang out while making your products."

Her hand flew to her mouth. "Are you sure?"

"It's the least I can do," he said with a grin. "Should I come by at noon tomorrow? What's your address?"

"I'll help too," said Mona and Leo in unison.

"I would help," said Julia, grimacing, "but I'm going to have a jam-packed week myself, getting the Fall Festival ready. As you can imagine, with Kristen's death and everything that happened in the case, I'm terribly behind, and"—she swallowed, her voice catching and tears glimmering in her eyes—"I want to make this the best Fall Festival the town's ever seen. For Kristen. She worked so hard on it."

"Don't feel the least bit bad," declared Vicki. "We're just so glad the Fall Festival is still on! I'm going to swing by the farmer's market on the way home and get the spices and some herbs—I'm not going to have enough in my herb garden for everything we have to make."

* * *

"So, when will Claire collect the first batch of bee venom?" Mona asked as she mashed pumpkin and sugar by the sink. The fragrant aroma of spiced cider filled Vicki's kitchen from a simmering pot on the back burner.

Vicki shrugged and cracked the window to toss a blueberry to

Sunny. "She installed the venom-collection system yesterday and said she'd check on it in a couple days to see if the bees seemed acclimated to it. But I'm going to donate October's venom and sell November's, so she did say I should get my first paycheck from it on the fifth of December. Between filling all these orders and that income stream, I should have enough to carry the business through the first quarter of next year!"

"And the store will be open the day after Thanksgiving so that people can buy Christmas presents!" sang Mona. "I've finally gotten the last details lined up."

The doorbell rang, and Vicki's heart skipped a beat.

"Is that James?" called Mona.

"I think so!"

Vicki ran to the front door just in time to see the delivery driver climb back into his truck. A wave of disappointment washed over her. But at least the rest of the supplies were here! She dragged in the boxes—some decorations for the booth and a mountain of ingredients to make more products. Even though the sale was over, more orders were coming in every day—the *Frugalicious* blog post was zinging its way around social media—and the Fall Festival was starting in just two days!

James had been given the whole week off, paid, as belated bereavement leave for Frank's death, and he'd come to Vicki's house every day to put in a full shift making products alongside Vicki and Mona. Leo was often there in the afternoons, after he got off work, and the four of them had established an easy, comfortable rapport—although Mona still wouldn't get up the courage to ask Leo out properly.

Vicki went back outside for the last box, and a grin spread across her face. James was pulling into the driveway in his silver sports car. He parked and headed toward her, holding a bouquet of peach roses.

"How's your mom doing?" she called.

"Her first bee-venom therapy with Dr. O'Rourke is officially in two weeks. She's really excited." He reached her and proffered the flowers. "Spotted these at the store and couldn't resist. They were nearly as pretty as you."

It felt like a swarm of giddy bees was buzzing in her stomach. She took the flowers and said, "Thank you! I love them! Let me get them in water."

She turned, but he caught her arm.

"Wait," he said, his voice suddenly husky.

She faced him, her head tilted, and he pulled her closer. "I've so enjoyed seeing you this week," he said, his voice low. "I hope you've had a good time too."

"I've loved every minute," she replied. The heady fragrance of the roses and the warmth of his gaze made her dizzy.

"Vicki Lawson, would you do me the honor of officially being my girlfriend?"

She could have lost herself in the deep pools of his blue eyes. "If you'll do *me* the honor of officially being my boyfriend."

He swept her into a passionate kiss, and she couldn't think of anything else but this perfect, beautiful moment.

Then a familiar voice warbled, "I love a happy ending!"

Vicki pulled back, startled to see Aunt Bee climbing out of her car. But it wasn't just Aunt Bee—Sheldon, Alana, and Tia all tumbled out, waving.

"We heard you're still buried under orders and need to get your products ready for the festival!" called Alana. "We're here to help!"

Aunt Bee held up a baggy. "I brought coupons to attach to Mona's jars of jam! But you won't need to put any of your products on sale, dear. They're flying off the shelves as it is!"

Then a police car turned onto the street and parked behind Aunt Bee. Vicki waved at Leo as he got out.

"I'm here to help too!" he said.

Vicki laughed aloud. "I don't know how to thank you all. I have the best friends, and I'm so lucky to have you on my team." She led them into the kitchen and began directing them as she cut the ends off the roses and put them in a vase of water. "Leo, would you mind grinding those herbs over there? Alana, would you measure out the other ingredients for Mona's pumpkin-spice jam? Tia, could you take some candid photos for the 'About' page on my online store? Aunt Bee, you could mix up a batch of my energizing scrub. The recipe is in that notebook on the counter. I've decided to call it *Rise & Shine!*"

"What about me?" asked James.

Vicki pulled him in for a brief, sweet kiss. When she released him, she said, "Can you help me package and address the orders that are going out today? I have printouts and packing materials on the table out back."

"I'd be delighted."

Vicki carried the vase of roses outside so that she could enjoy them as they packed orders at the folding table that overlooked Sunny's little duck pond. Sunny waddled up to Vicki, and Vicki laughed and said, "I forgot your blueberries, didn't I?"

Aunt Bee passed the bowl of blueberries through the window, and Vicki tossed a berry into the duck pond. Sunny ran for the little pool, her white tail feathers flapping in the breeze, and dove into the water.

Vicki taped the first box shut, and as she reached for the next packing slip, her hand brushed James's. He threaded his fingers through hers as a gust of wind blew through the yard, sending a shiver down Vicki's spine. A cascade of red leaves floated through the air, falling softly to the ground like snowflakes. With a laugh, James scooped Vicki into his arms and spun her around. Then he set her gently down and caressed her cheek and pulled her into a kiss so tender and perfect she thought her heart might burst.

READY FOR MORE?

*B*ook 3 from Cooking up Murder available soon...

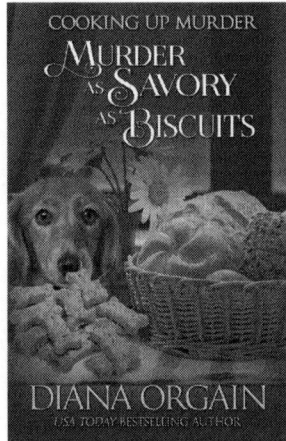

Click here to get your copy now.

PREVIEW OF MURDER AS SAVORY AS BISCUITS

CHAPTER 1

*T*here was a spring in Leo Lawson's step as he walked the hay-bale-filled passageways of the Fall Festival at Magnolia Falls.

Today was the day.

He was finally going to ask Mona out. He'd known her since they were kids. Because she was his sister's best friend, he'd always figured they couldn't ever be more than platonic. But the time had come. He couldn't stand the torment anymore. He had to ask her.

All around, the sights and sounds and smells of the Fall Festival tugged at him. Homemade pies. Locally brewed beer. Handcrafted furniture. The tangy scent of barbecue hit his nostrils, and his stomach rumbled. But no—he would not be lured away by Bandit Bob's BBQ or their fine pulled-pork sandwiches. He was a man on a mission.

He headed straight to the Jammin Honey booth, where both Mona and his sister would be. Over the top of a hay bale, he spotted a colorful cowgirl hat that could only belong to Mona's eccentric Aunt Bee.

Abort! He couldn't do this with Aunt Bee here. She was wonderful, but she had a way of commandeering the room—and was never, ever shy about expressing her thoughts.

Leo spun on his heel to make a run for it, but Aunt Bee had spotted him.

She grabbed his elbow. She sure was fast on her feet for an octogenarian.

"Leo! I knew you'd make it. Have you had a chance to grab our latest coupon?"

Aunt Bee ran the local Coupon Clippers club, and she'd stop at nothing to get a great deal on a purchase.

"I've got the latest steal for you, hon," she said, squeezing his bicep as if she were juicing a lemon.

"What's that, Aunt Bee?" he asked, untangling himself from her grip.

"It's a two-for-one over at Greta Cox's beer booth." She gave him a direct look and waggled her eyebrows.

He laughed aloud. "That sounds great. Right up my alley. But I'm on duty."

"Well, save it for later," she said, turning her attention to the aisle, no doubt looking for her next catch.

Leo smiled despite himself and approached the Jammin Honey booth. Vicki, his sister and the world's best purveyor of honeybee products, was chatting with some customers, but he didn't see Mona.

Where could she be? The anxious tug in his belly surprised him.

Vicki spotted him and waved him over. She finished chatting with her customer, and then picked up a couple packets and held them out toward Leo. "Got some samples for you."

He gave her a look. "Haven't I tried all your stuff before?"

Leo tended to be Vicki's guinea pig for all her body scrubs and face products. Some had turned out great, while others had been a little questionable. She'd once turned his face *green*.

Vicki laughed. "You can never have too many scrubs."

"I'm here to eat." Leo patted his abs and looked around. "Where's Mona?"

Vicki smirked at him. "Mona doesn't need to be here to feed you. Help yourself." She pointed toward the samples of homemade jams and jellies on the gluten-free bread Mona loved so much. Leo picked up a couple and stuffed them in his mouth.

"So . . . where is she?" he asked.

Vicki put her hands on her hips. "Aha! Are you finally going to ask her out?"

"I'd like to," Leo said. "And I'd like to do it without you being so nosy about it."

Vicki pumped her fist triumphantly. "You know I want my best friend to be my sister-in-law. Get to it."

"Well, where is she, for crying out loud?" Leo asked, exasperated.

"She'll be here soon. She was running over to talk to some of the people at the cheese booth to see if they could pair some dry cheeses with her jam."

Leo nodded. Mona was a workaholic. It was one of the things he liked about her. Before long, he glimpsed her honey-colored hair through the crowd, and a warm feeling filled his chest. A shy smile crossed Mona's face when she saw him, and the warm feeling grew.

"Hey!" Mona said. "Are you hungry? I've wrangled some cheese samples." She unpackaged the bundle she was carrying, and Leo dug into some cheese and grapes.

"Well . . . I had another reason for coming," he said when he swallowed. "Although this cheese is excellent."

Mona looked at him expectantly, and Vicki ducked down as if she were digging more product out of the boxes underneath the table.

He paused, then blurted, "I was wondering if maybe you had time Wednesday afternoon. I have the day off. I wanted to hike up to the falls, maybe have a picnic."

Mona bit her lip. "I'd love that," she said, her voice squeaking. "Wednesday it is."

They looked at each other awkwardly, and suddenly Leo didn't know what to do with himself. He wanted to kiss her, but that would be too much too fast. Like an idiot, he fought the impulse to stick his hand out to shake hers.

She'd agreed to a date, not a business deal, for crying out loud.

Clumsily, he stuck his hands in his pockets.

"I can pack the basket," Mona said, her cheeks reddening. "I'll get some more of these cheeses, and maybe a little wine?"

He nodded. "That sounds great." From his pocket, he fished out the coupon Aunt Bee had given him and offered it to Mona. "Oh, I have a two-for. Two beers for the price of one, but I can't drink right now—I'm on duty." He tapped the police-issued radio strapped to his shoulder.

Mona accepted the coupon. "Thank you! Vicki and I will have some after we clean up our booth—we'll toast to you." She gave him a big wink, then seemed flustered about it. "It's . . . the last day of the festival. The booth has done really well, so it'll be good to have a way to celebrate."

"Good. I'm very glad," he said. "Now I need to go and patrol—keep this rowdy Fall Festival crowd under control."

As if on cue, a country band took the stage and started crooning a cover of "I Cross My Heart." In front of the stage, couples paired off to slow dance.

Leo and Mona exchanged looks. He wished he could stay and dance with her, but he needed to make the rounds. And it wasn't like he could ask her to slow dance yet—he'd just asked her on a first date!

Two teenage boys whizzed by them, a vendor in hot pursuit.

"Shoplifter!" yelled the vendor.

Adrenaline surged in Leo, and he bolted after the little thieves, shouting over his shoulder, "See you Wednesday!"

PREVIEW OF MURDER AS SAVORY AS BISCUITS

CHAPTER 2

*L*eo and Mona chatted happily as they climbed Magnolia Falls Trail. Mona had thrown her hair back in a ponytail and wore hiking boots, leggings that hugged her shapely form, and a long-sleeved workout tunic. Leo's heart pounded when he looked at her. Even in athletic clothes and without a stitch of makeup, she was so beautiful.

At the top of the trail, should he take her behind the waterfall and kiss her? People did that sort of thing in romantic movies. But this was only their first date. He didn't want to make her uncomfortable.

She tucked a loose strand of hair behind her ear and gave him a smile that made him dizzy. He took a step forward without thinking and almost tumbled off the side of the trail. He caught himself on a tree branch and glanced down at the ravine. He needed to pay better attention. A fall like that wouldn't kill him—it would be more of a long, inevitable roll than a sheer drop—but it would sure hurt.

And mortally wound his pride, no doubt.

Once they got to the top, they snapped a few selfies and texted them to Vicki, then set up their picnic on a long, flat rock near the roar of the waterfall.

Leo opened up the backpack and pulled out a blanket that Mona had packed. He laid it out, and they both plopped on top of it.

"I think I'm getting a blister," Mona said, taking off her shoes.

"Let me take a look," Leo said, grabbing for her foot.

She pulled back. "No way. My feet are sticky and gross."

"I don't care," he said, chuckling. "I did a tour in Afghanistan—I've seen sticky and gross feet before, believe me."

After a moment's hesitation, she let him look at her feet. He peeled off her sweaty sock and examined the back of her heel.

"Yup, you're working up a blister. Better air them out a little bit." Then he gave her a crooked grin. "I'd give you a foot massage, but your feet *are* kinda stinky and gross."

She kicked his legs with her bare feet. "Shut up, you big oaf. I'm sure your feet are way stinkier and grosser."

He kicked off his boots. "They're supposed to be. I'm an oaf."

He uncorked the bottle of wine and poured her a glass. Despite the late-autumn chill, the sun was warm in the sky, and the wine tasted a bit like heaven. He felt himself relax, starting from his shoulders. Mona was nervously chatting about the progress on the shop—her store had burned down a few months ago, and it was scheduled for its grand opening the day after Thanksgiving—but he was so intoxicated looking at her beautiful profile that he didn't really hear a word.

He scooched closer to her until their hips touched. He wrapped an arm around her waist, and she stiffened, suddenly going quiet. His breath hitched. Had he misread her signals? Did she not want him to touch her?

Mind racing, he released her. "I'm—"

A loud rustling in the bushes stopped him short.

Leo jumped to his feet as a golden retriever tore out of the brambles.

"What on earth!" Mona shrieked.

The dog wailed loudly and charged at them. Was that *blood* on its fur? Was it rabid? Had it been attacked by something?

Instinctively, Leo stepped between Mona and the dog. He regretted taking off his boots. Trouble never seemed to be far away—a string of bad luck seemed to have stalked the town of Magnolia Falls recently. The dog barked and whined mournfully.

"He's hurt," Mona said, moving toward the retriever.

"Hold up, hold up," Leo said. "Don't touch it."

The dog barked at them sharply, then tore off back into the woods. Leo and Mona glanced at each other. A moment later, the dog's snout poked through the bushes, and it barked again, as if beckoning them.

"He wants us to follow him," Mona said.

"You stay here," he told her, tying his laces.

"Not on your life," she said, sticking her feet into her boots. "I'm going with you."

"You're stubborn."

Mona snorted. "You like it."

He swallowed. She was right. And maybe her retort meant she *had* wanted him to put his arm around her?

She tore off after the dog, with Leo in hot pursuit.

The dog raced through the bushes, howling as it led them down a narrow path toward the bottom of the falls. A sickening pit opened up in Leo's stomach. This was trouble—he knew it. He grabbed for his shoulder radio and realized he hadn't brought it along. Of course he hadn't. It was his day off. He wasn't in uniform.

The dog galloped to the far side of a clearing. Once there, it stopped short and growled.

Leo reached for his ankle holster. Thank goodness, some habits died hard, even when he was off-duty in a small town.

"Stay here and call 911," Leo said to Mona. She pulled out her cell phone and dialed.

Leo reached the dog, now on point, and called out, "Police."

The silence was deafening. Then the dog began to cry. It whined and whimpered, finally laying its head on its forepaws.

"What is it, boy?" Leo asked. But somehow, he already knew.

He holstered his weapon and shoved aside the brush.

A body lay in the foliage—a man wearing a suit drenched in blood.

PREVIEW OF MURDER AS SAVORY AS BISCUITS

CHAPTER 3

"Not exactly the way I was hoping our first date would go," Mona said under her breath, looking anywhere except at the body in the brush.

Leo nodded, sighing heavily. He'd just gotten off the phone with dispatch, and they were sending a crime-scene unit. The dog whined, not budging from the man's side.

Yup, this year sure had brought a whole spree of bad luck to the town of Magnolia Falls. Their small community hadn't seen a murder in ten years, and then an arsonist had burned down Mona's store, killing someone in the process. Just a few months later, a pair of selfish siblings had murdered two people in a bid to keep themselves from being disinherited, and Leo's sister Vicki had been caught up in the middle of the investigation.

And now he'd found a body in the woods.

The dog pushed his nose into the man's face and whimpered mournfully.

"Come here, boy," Leo said, worried the dog was going to contaminate the crime scene. The dog whined again and limped over to Leo.

"Is he hurt?" Mona asked.

Leo bent down by the retriever. Its face was covered in blood. From the dead man, maybe? The dog had been sniffing around him quite a bit. But upon further examination, he found a stab wound in the dog's front right leg.

"He's been stabbed," Leo said.

"The man?" Mona asked.

"The dog."

"You poor thing!" Mona cried, kneeling. The dog's tail thumped half-heartedly. While Mona fawned over the injured dog, Leo took another look at the body. What he saw chilled him to his core, and a protective instinct rushed over him.

"Oh my gosh! Mona, stay away from the dog!" he snapped, spinning around. The retriever was lying on its back, and Mona was rubbing its belly.

"Why?" she asked.

"This man . . . he was bit . . . in the throat . . ." Leo stood upright despite a wave of nausea.

Mona furrowed her eyebrows like he was crazy. "You think this sweet little guy killed him? There's no way."

"Mona, I don't know, but it kinda looks that way. Please, just back away from the dog."

She crossed her arms and stood up. "There's no way this dog killed that guy."

"Leo!" a voice called from beyond the trees.

"Over this way!" Leo called back, waving his arms as a handful of officers from the station's crime-scene unit trudged past the tree line.

"This dog is sweet," Mona insisted, still rubbing the retriever's belly. "If it hurt that man like that, it wasn't the aggressor. Maybe the guy was the one who stabbed him, or something."

Leo eyed her, then turned and shook hands with his fellow officers and briefly explained how they'd come across the scene.

One of the younger officers, Reynolds, squinted toward the body. "Shoot, I know him."

"Who is he?" Leo asked.

"Jonathan Darsey," Reynolds said. "Business guy."

"I could have guessed that from the suit," Leo said.

"Oh, I know the name," said Officer Truff, the oldest member of the group. "He's new to town, isn't he?"

"Yeah," said Reynolds. "Well, sort of. He's from Pigeon Hollow originally. Lives somewhere in the county—I've heard it's a big estate, but I don't know where it is. But he just bought that big lot on the edge of town for his factory. What are they making—boots or something?"

"Speaking of which," Mona said, stepping into the circle of officers. "What's a guy doing dressed like that in the middle of the woods?"

"Probably not hiking." Leo crossed his arms. "The dog does seem to know him, though."

"Doesn't take a genius to see that the dog bit him and that he bled out," Reynolds said. "Dog's gonna have to be put down."

"Don't jump to conclusions, rookie," replied Truff. "We're going to need an autopsy."

"Seriously?" Reynolds questioned. "The dog is covered in his blood, and that wound on his neck is obviously a bite mark."

Mona put her hands on her hips. "This dog didn't bite him!"

Reynolds shot a questioning look in her direction. "Unless the autopsy results show something crazy, it seems pretty straightforward to me."

"No, it doesn't," Mona retorted. "The guy's in the middle of the woods in a suit. No one walks their dog like that. Look at his shoes. It doesn't make sense. And someone even stabbed the poor dog in the leg."

"I don't know," Officer Truff said, his eyes kind. "If I had to guess, the dog attacked the victim, the victim stabbed back in self-defense, and its owner ran off when they realized their dog had killed the man."

Mona's hands shook, and she bit her lip like she might be about to burst into angry tears.

"Okay, let's slow down a bit, fellas," Leo said. "I think Mona might have a point. The scene is odd, and the dog hasn't shown any signs of aggression. Let's be sure we do a thorough sweep of the scene."

"What about the dog?" Reynolds asked.

"I guess we take it to the pound after we get a cast of its mouth to confirm whether or not it actually bit the victim," said Truff. "Then, after the autopsy, we'll know whether it needs to be put down or not."

Mona grabbed Leo's arm and shook her head, eyes wide. "They'll mistreat it," she whispered harshly. "They think it's a killer."

Leo sighed and glanced from Mona to the crime-scene unit to the retriever. He surprised himself with the next words out of his mouth. "I'll take the dog. It needs to be seen by a vet, and there's one near my house."

Reynolds stared at him, agape. "You're really going to watch this dog while this case is being investigated?"

"I don't see why not," Leo said. "I've got plenty of room, and my yard is fenced in."

Truff shrugged. "Let me check in with the chief and see if it's okay for the dog to come home with you, but he'll probably be glad he doesn't have to deal with the idiot who runs animal control. You three start on the crime scene, and I'll head back to the cruiser and radio the chief."

Leo looked down at the retriever. It was lying on the ground, head propped up on its front paws, occasionally letting out a soft whine.

Panic flared in Leo's chest. What had he just committed to?

Great going, Leo.

But then Mona threaded her fingers through his and squeezed his hand. A giddy smile flashed across his face.

This would be fine. This had been a *good* idea. If the dog was innocent, they couldn't very well let it be swept off to the pound. It might get euthanized prematurely there.

Mona sat next to the dog and rubbed its ears, murmuring in soothing tones. Though Leo kept a sharp eye on the retriever for any signs of aggression, it just lay there, its tail occasionally thumping from side to side.

A few minutes later, Officer Truff reappeared on the path, shooting Leo a thumbs-up. "You're good to take the dog," he called. "Just wait a few minutes for the forensics team. They need to swab the blood on the dog's fur and take a cast of its mouth."

When the forensics team arrived, they did their job quickly and efficiently, and the dog appeared no more aggressive even when three people were poking and prodding him and prying his mouth open to take the cast.

"See," Mona said quietly.

Leo couldn't help but agree with her. This wasn't a vicious dog. If it had attacked, it must have been severely provoked.

The dog willingly followed Mona down the trail, and she spread her picnic blanket across Leo's back seat and coaxed the dog into the car. He hoped the picnic blanket would be enough and that he wouldn't find bloodstains on his seats later, but he didn't breathe a word of that concern to Mona.

"Hey," he said as he made the first turn. "Can you call ahead and let the vet know we're coming?"

"Great idea!" She dialed, and after a brief conversation, she hung up and said, "They'll see us as soon as we get there."

Sure enough, they were ushered to an exam room as soon as they brought the dog in. The vet swept into the room, and Leo was struck by his gentle demeanor. But he cast a suspicious glance at Leo and Mona.

"I understand we have a stab wound?" the vet asked.

"That's right," said Mona. "On his front leg."

The vet bent down and scratched the dog's chin, then inspected the stab wound. "Blood on his fur, too," he murmured. He looked up at Leo and Mona. "What happened?"

"We're not sure," said Leo. "I'm a detective. We found the dog at a crime scene, and I'm taking care of him while the case is under investigation."

The vet eyed Leo as if he didn't quite believe him, so Leo pulled out his badge and held it out for inspection. The vet studied it and nodded, then stood and stuck out his hand. "I'm Dr. Mansour. Pleased to meet you."

Leo returned the handshake.

Dr. Mansour looked back down at the retriever and said, "All right, big guy, should we get you up on the exam table?"

The dog's tail thumped.

Dr. Mansour and Mona eased the dog onto the table, and then Dr. Mansour gave the dog a shot to numb the pain.

The retriever hardly flinched.

"We're going to clean the wound and then stitch it up," Dr.

Mansour said. "He did really good with that shot. Are you a good boy?"

Leo and Mona sat while the vet finished treating the wound. When he finished, the dog raised its head and gave the vet kisses on his chin.

With a chuckle, Dr. Mansour said, "Really great dog. Some dogs I have to drug pretty heavily to get them to sit still for stitches, or even bring in a few techs to hold them down—or both. I've been bitten and knocked over I can't tell you how many times. A tech will be back in a moment with a couple days of pain medication. Make sure he doesn't overgroom the stitches, or we'll have to put a cone on him. Any questions?"

"Just one," said Leo. "So, nothing you've seen would make you think the dog has any aggressive tendencies?"

"Not at all. Why?"

"We're ruling him out as a suspect in a crime."

"Hmm." Dr. Mansour reached out and ruffled the retriever's ears. "What's the situation?"

"Dead guy," said Leo with a grimace.

Dr. Mansour's eyes widened. "With a dog bite?"

"It looked like there was a bite to the throat. Body was found in the woods. Dog led us to him."

Mona added, "The dog seemed sad."

Dr. Mansour nodded slowly. "Well, almost every dog can be pushed to violence in the right circumstances—just like almost any person can be. Some dogs will be violent if they feel threatened. Even more will be violent if their person is threatened. But if he led you to the body and seemed sad, I'd say with a fair degree of certainty that he's not your biter. I'd guess you'll discover that the victim was his owner." He reached out again and gave the retriever one more pat on the head. "Poor thing. Let me know if you need anything else, all right?"

"Thank you for all your help," said Mona.

Dr. Mansour nodded and left the room, leaving Leo alone with Mona and the dog.

"See?" Mona said with a self-satisfied look.

Leo sighed. "I agree with you. I really do. But you know what that scene looked like, and I don't want you to get too upset if they wind up putting him down."

Mona nodded slowly. "I understand. But those other officers just seemed so quick to jump to conclusions."

"You know, I didn't see a knife on Darsey," Leo said. "Which probably means someone else was at that crime scene. It's possible the knife will be found by the other officers—I didn't have much of a chance to look around, because we left before they finished processing the evidence. But if Darsey stabbed the dog, it's going to come off looking like he was trying to defend himself against a mauling."

Mona sighed. "It just doesn't feel right, Leo. I mean, I'm a big animal person, I know. So, I'm sure it seems like I'm biased. But just look at him."

Leo glanced down at the retriever that was now curled up on the floor, looking impossibly dejected.

"Plus," said Mona. "He's a golden retriever. They're family-friendly dogs. I've never met an aggressive one."

That was a fair point. Had Leo seen a single biting incident in a golden retriever in his time on the force? He didn't think so.

A vet tech returned, handing Leo a bag. "The meds will help the poor guy with pain," he said. "Wrap one pill up into some bologna or ham to get him to eat it. Once in the morning and once at night. Give him the first one tonight before you go to bed, and he should be okay. You're going to want to be careful when bathing him, too. His stitches are fine to get wet, but you'll want to be very gentle around the wound."

Leo nodded. "Yeah, he's going to need a bath, for sure."

"Last thing." The tech held up a wand of some kind. "Mind if I scan him for a microchip? See if we can track down the owner that way?"

"Please do," said Leo.

The tech waved the wand over the dog's neck and shoulders. "We've got a chip!" he exclaimed. "I'll call the chip company and get you the owner's information."

At checkout, Leo cringed at the six hundred dollar bill. Maybe the station would reimburse him, but he doubted it. He'd volunteered to take care of the dog, so he was probably going to be stuck with the bill. He sighed and handed his credit card to the receptionist.

"Good boy, who's a good boy? Who's a good boy?" crooned Mona behind him. He glanced over his shoulder. She was kneeling down on the floor, scratching the dog behind the ears. The dog's tail was wagging as it rubbed its head against her arms.

"That poor thing," the receptionist said as she ran Leo's card. "Why would someone hurt such a sweet dog?"

Leo shrugged. He was still thinking about the massive credit card bill he was going to have to pay at the end of the month.

Then the vet tech came into the room, frowning. "So, the dog is chipped, but the company said that there's no owner information— that the owner called in last Friday asking for all their information to be taken off the chip's record. They weren't able to give me more than that."

Last Friday? Leo frowned. Odd. That was before the time of death. Even if the owner had planned to sic the dog on Jonathan, surely they hadn't planned on leaving it out in the woods as evidence.

He and Mona headed out, and the dog walked right at their heels. It didn't even need a leash.

Leo dropped Mona off at her house, and she smiled brightly at him before she climbed out of the car and headed toward her door. When she was safely in the house, he let out a long sigh. The dog gingerly picked its way over the console and into the passenger seat.

Leo absentmindedly reached out and scratched the retriever's head.

What in the world did I get myself into?

KEEP READING...

❦

To Continue...

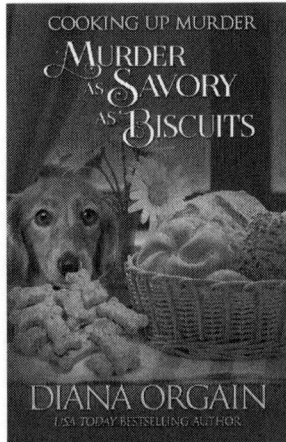

Click here to get your copy now.

GET SELECT DIANA ORGAIN TITLES FOR FREE

uilding a relationship with my readers is one the things I enjoy best. I occasionally send out messages about new releases, special offers, discount codes and other bits of news relating to my various series.

And for a limited time, I'll send you copy of BUNDLE OF TROUBLE: Book 1 in the MATERNAL INSTINCTS MYSTERY SERIES.

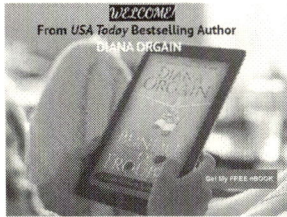

Join now

ABOUT THE AUTHOR

Diana Orgain is the bestselling author of the *Maternal Instincts Mystery Series*, the *Love or Money Mystery Series*, and the *Roundup Crew Mysteries*. She is the co-author of NY Times Bestselling *Scrapbooking Mystery Series* with Laura Childs. For a complete listing of books, as well as excerpts and contests, and to connect with Diana:

Visit Diana's website at www.dianaorgain.com.

Join Diana reader club and newsletter and get Free books here

Made in the USA
Middletown, DE
02 August 2021